LUZ
MAKES a
SPLASH

Kids Can Press acknowledges the financial support of the Government of Ontario, through the Ontario Media Development Corporation's Ontario Book Initiative; the Ontario Arts Council; the Canada Council for the Arts; and the Government of Canada, through the BPIDP, for our publishing activity.

Published in Canada by
Kids Can Press Ltd.
25 Dockside Drive
Toronto, ON M5A 0B5

Published in the U.S. by
Kids Can Press Ltd.
2250 Military Road
Tonawanda, NY 14150

www.kidscanpress.com

Edited by Karen Li and Samantha Swenson
Designed by Claudia Dávila and Rachel Di Salle

The hardcover edition of this book is smyth sewn casebound.
The paperback edition of this book is limp sewn with a drawn-on cover.
Manufactured in Shen Zhen, Guang Dong, P.R. China, in 5/2012 by Printplus Limited.

CM 12 0 9 8 7 6 5 4 3 2 1
CM PA 12 0 9 8 7 6 5 4 3 2 1

FSC
www.fsc.org
MIX
Paper from
responsible sources
FSC® C018479

Library and Archives Canada Cataloguing in Publication

Dávila, Claudia
Luz makes a splash / by Claudia Dávila.

ISBN 978-1-55453-762-4 (bound) ISBN 978-1-55453-769-3 (pbk.)

I. Title. II. Series: Dávila, Claudia. Future according to Luz.

PS8607.A95285L87 2012   jC813'.6   C2011-906930-X

Kids Can Press is a **CORUS**™ Entertainment company

LUZ MAKES a SPLASH

By
Claudia
Dávila

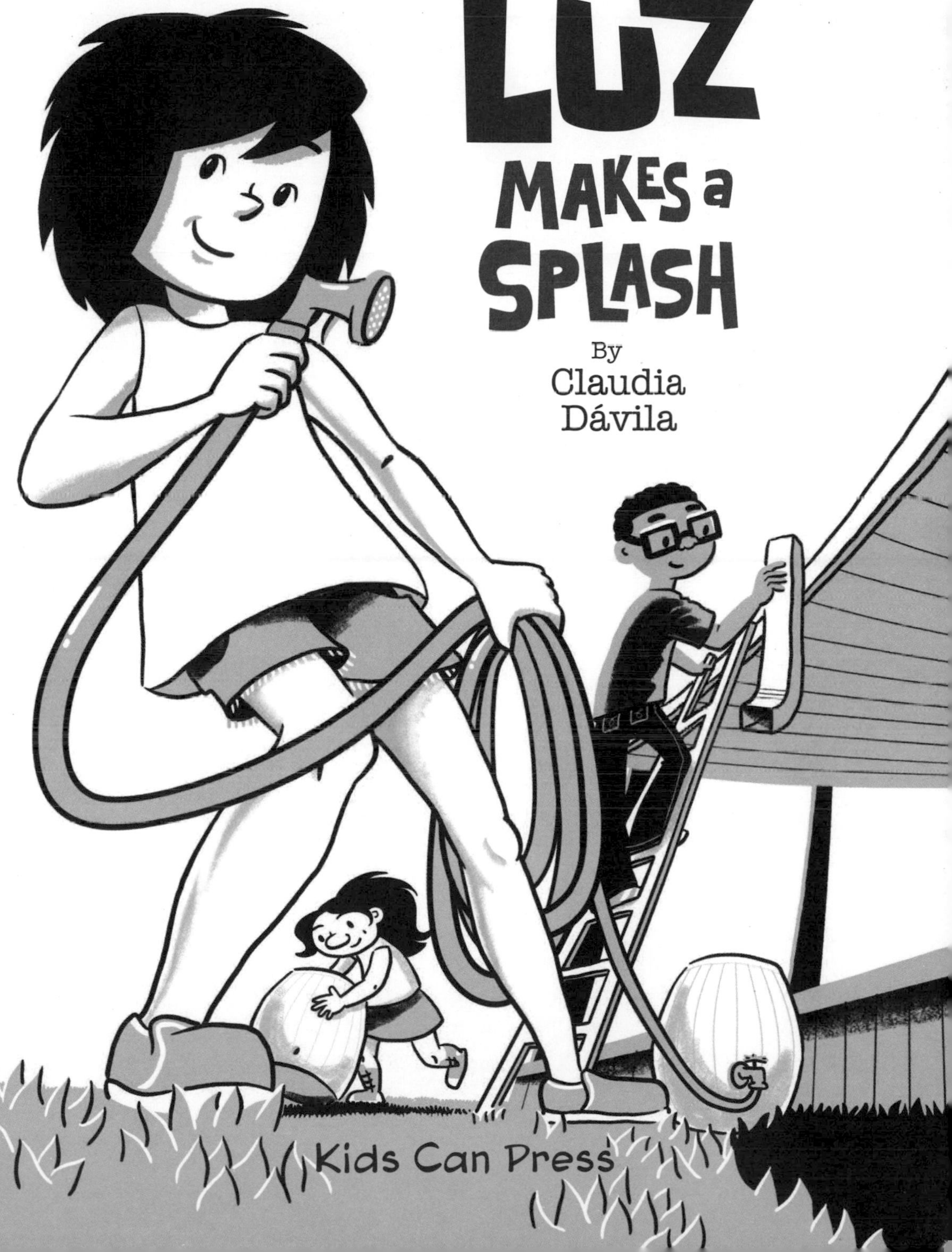

Kids Can Press

For Michael and Yolanda

Contents

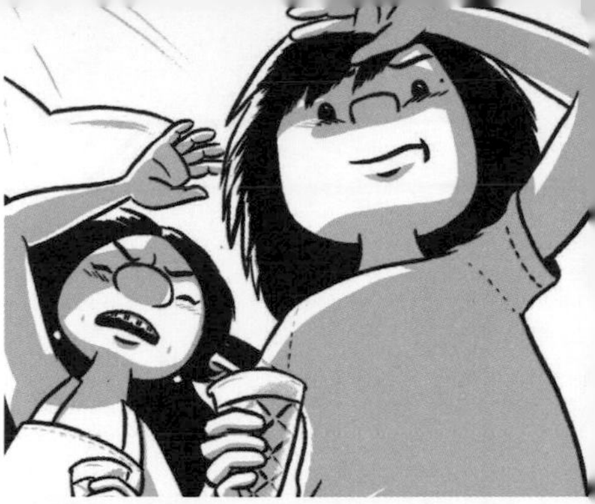

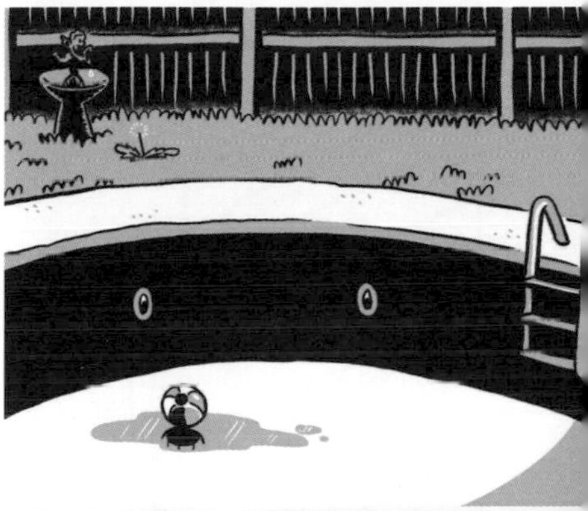

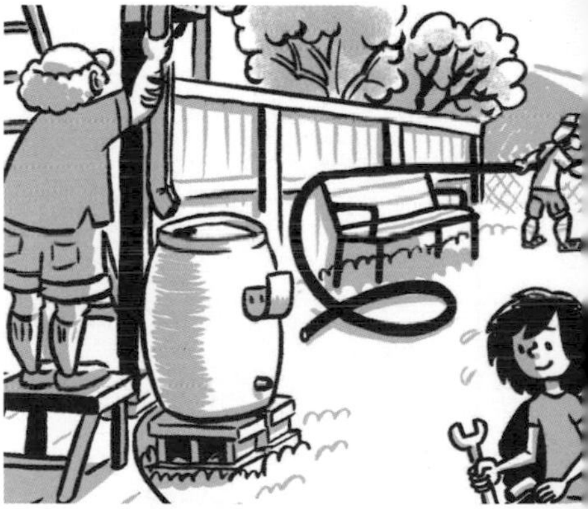

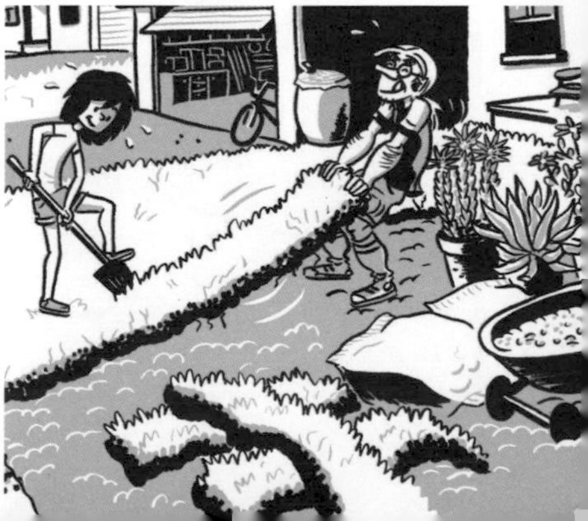

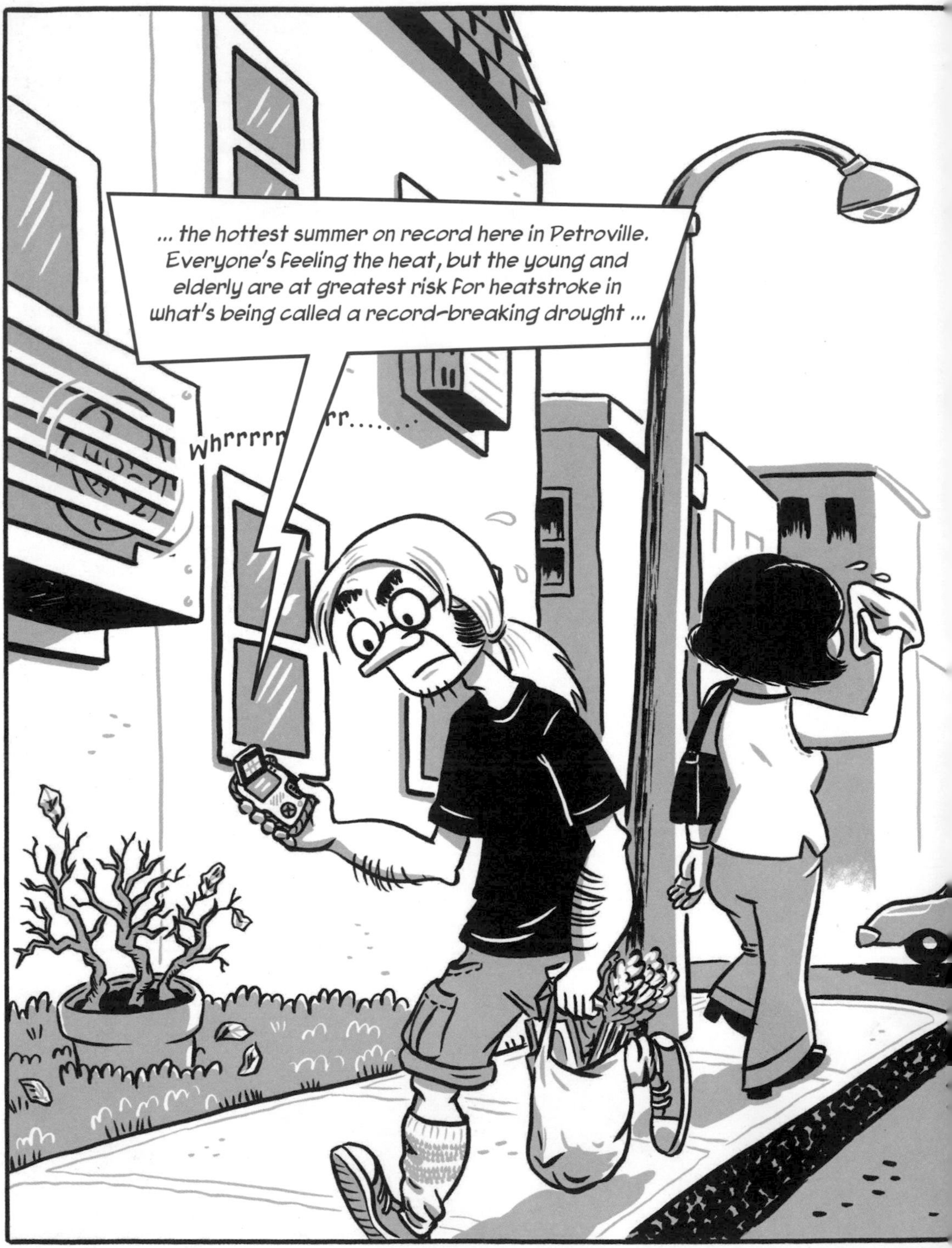
... the hottest summer on record here in Petroville. Everyone's feeling the heat, but the young and elderly are at greatest risk for heatstroke in what's being called a record-breaking drought ...
Whrrrrr rr........

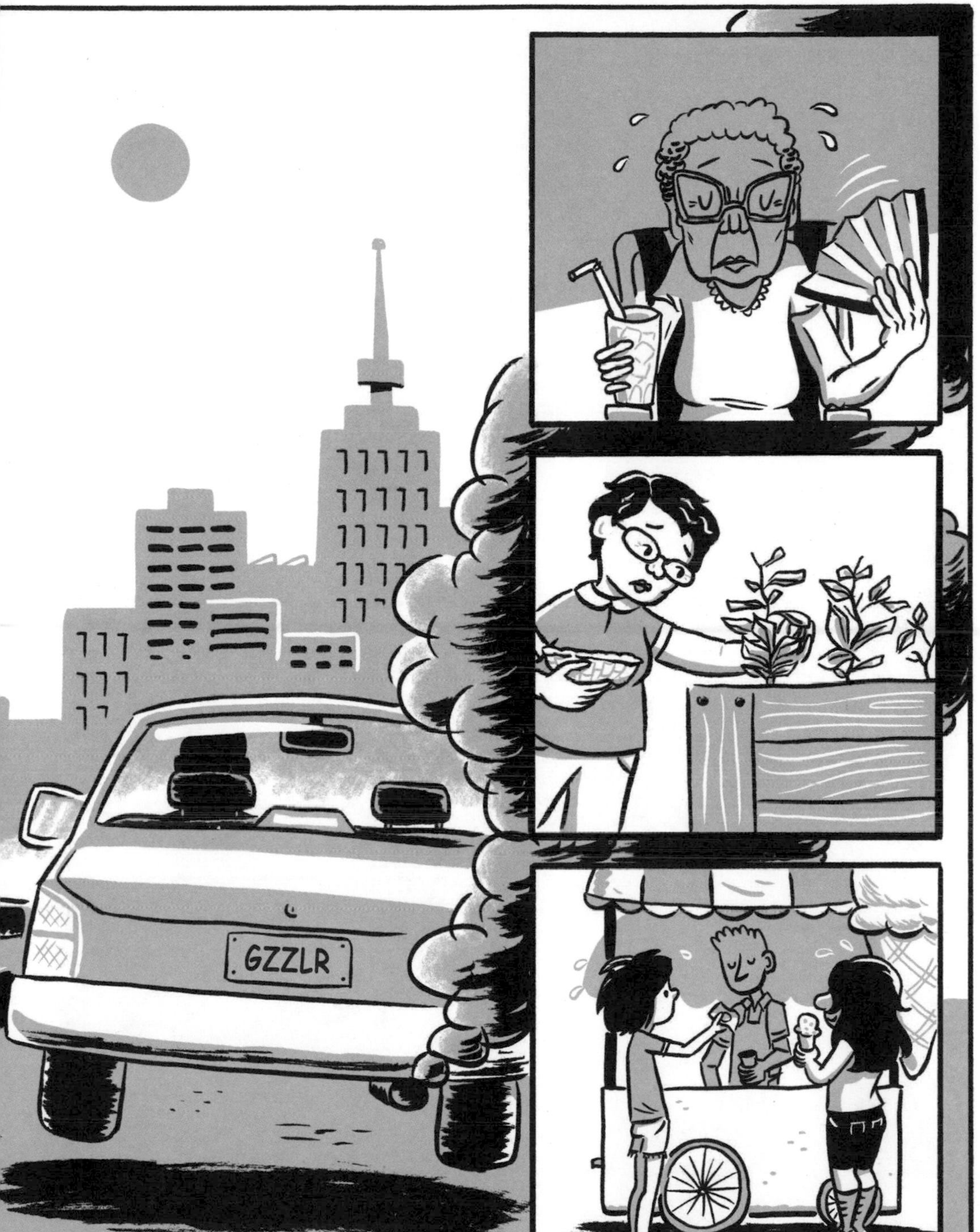
GZZLR

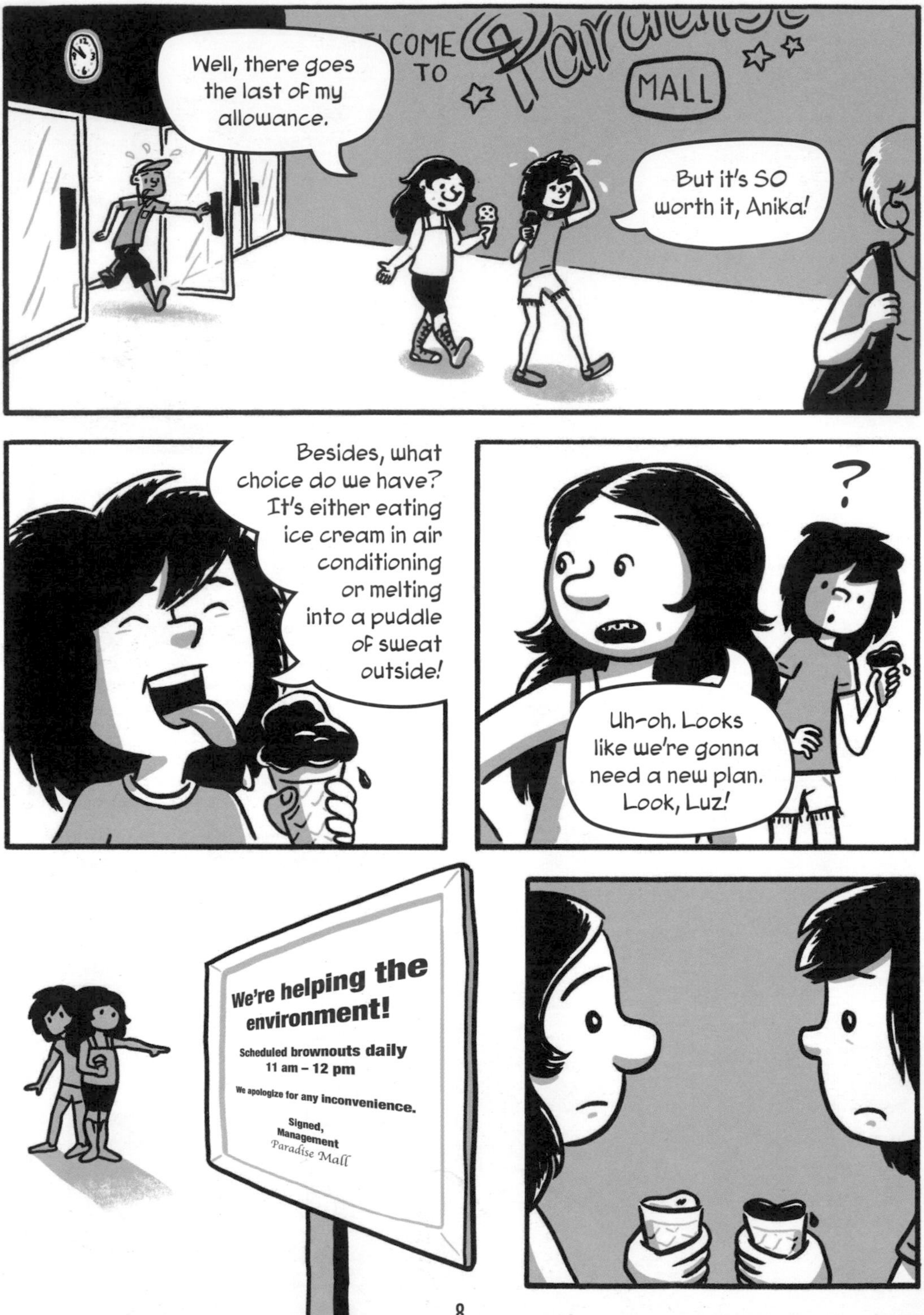
WELCOME TO Paradise MALL
Well, there goes the last of my allowance.
But it's SO worth it, Anika!
Besides, what choice do we have? It's either eating ice cream in air conditioning or melting into a puddle of sweat outside!
?
Uh-oh. Looks like we're gonna need a new plan. Look, Luz!
We're helping the environment!
Scheduled brownouts daily
11 am – 12 pm
We apologize for any inconvenience.
Signed,
Management
Paradise Mall

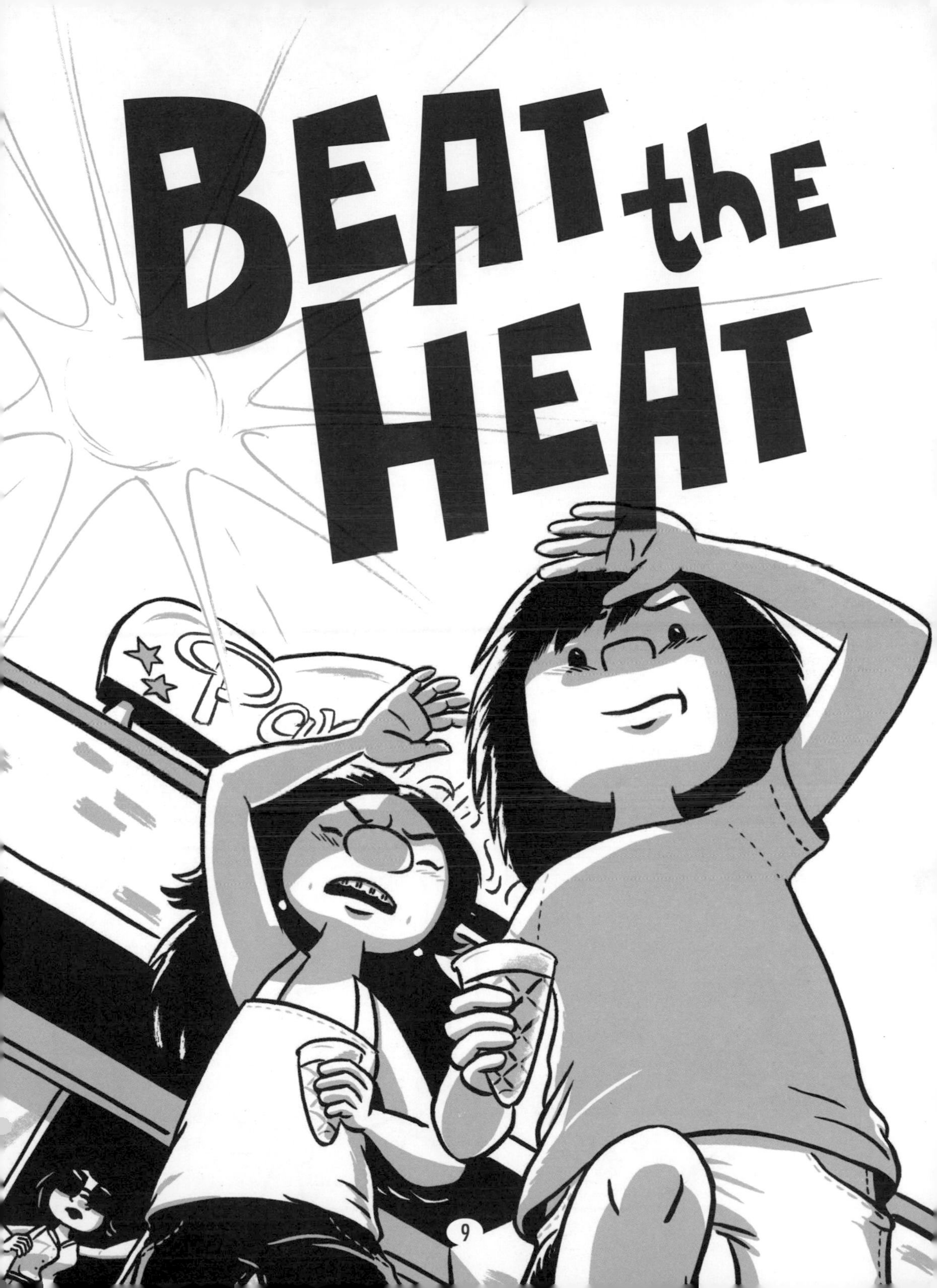
BEAT the HEAT

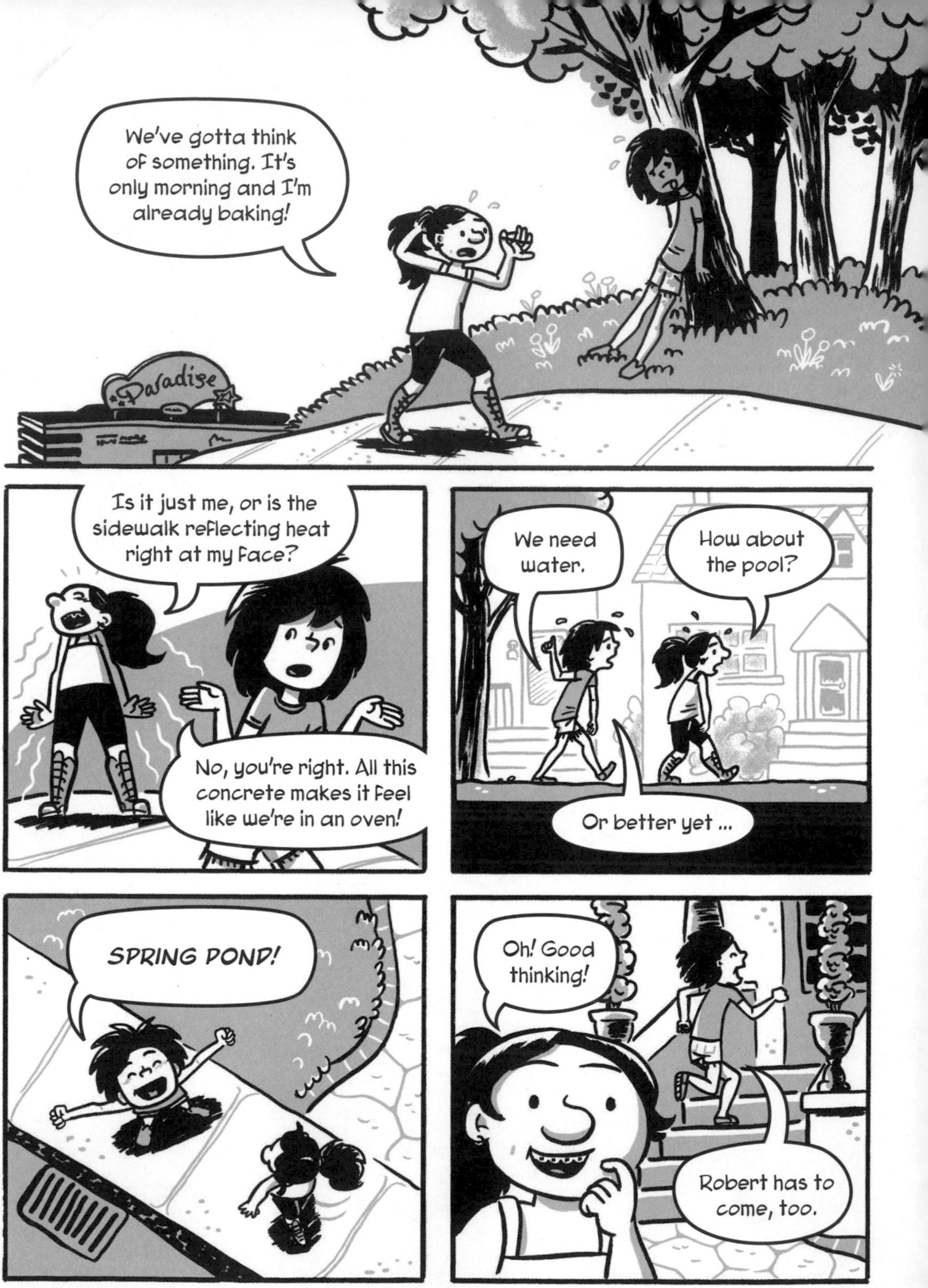
We've gotta think of something. It's only morning and I'm already baking!
Paradise
Is it just me, or is the sidewalk reflecting heat right at my face?
No, you're right. All this concrete makes it feel like we're in an oven!
We need water.
How about the pool?
Or better yet ...
SPRING POND!
Oh! Good thinking!
Robert has to come, too.

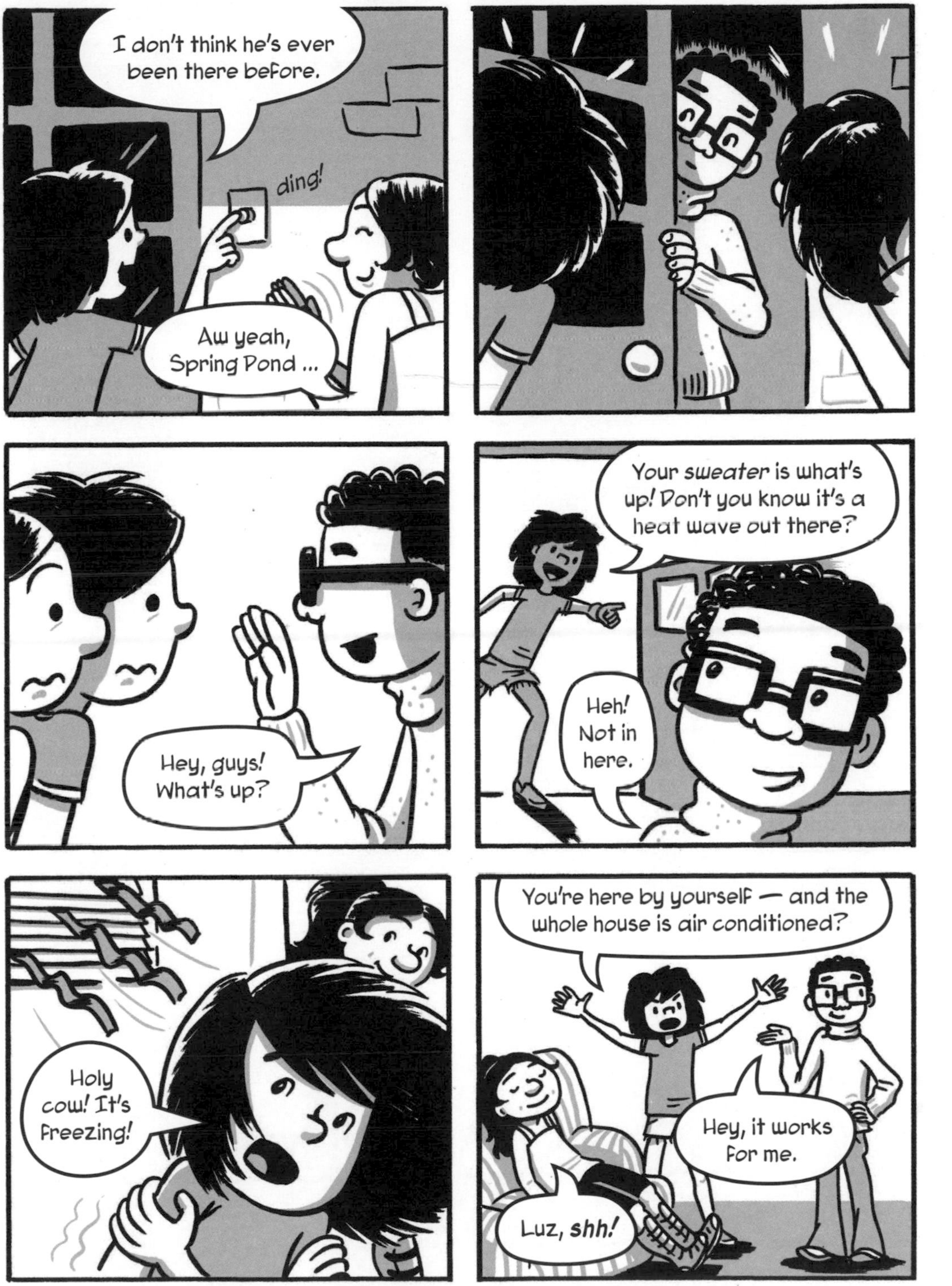
I don't think he's ever been there before.
ding!
Aw yeah, Spring Pond ...
Hey, guys! What's up?
Your *sweater* is what's up! Don't you know it's a heat wave out there?
Heh! Not in here.
Holy cow! It's freezing!
You're here by yourself — and the whole house is air conditioned?
Hey, it works for me.
Luz, **shh!**

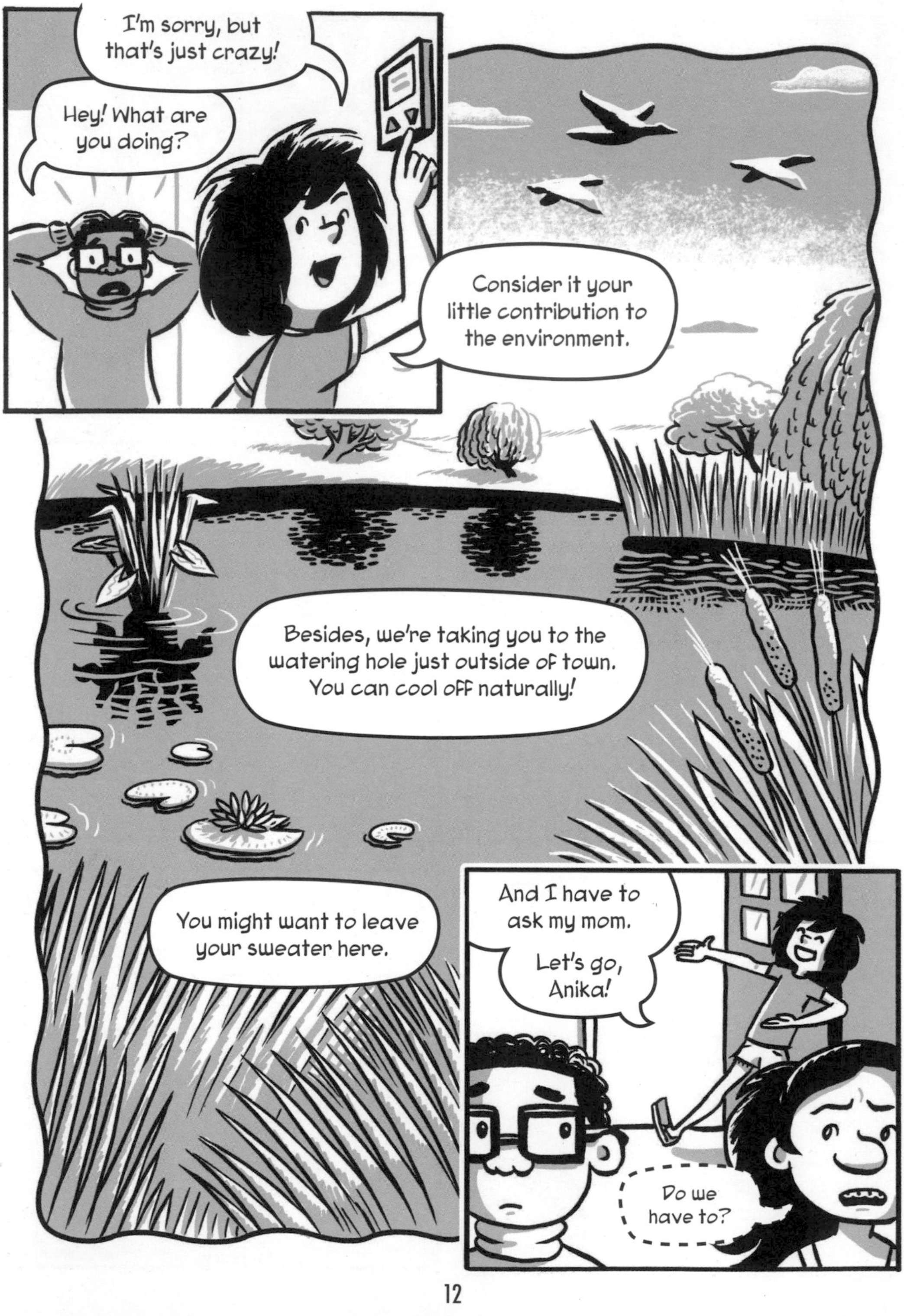
I'm sorry, but that's just crazy!
Hey! What are you doing?
Consider it your little contribution to the environment.
Besides, we're taking you to the watering hole just outside of town. You can cool off naturally!
You might want to leave your sweater here.
And I have to ask my mom.
Let's go, Anika!
Do we have to?

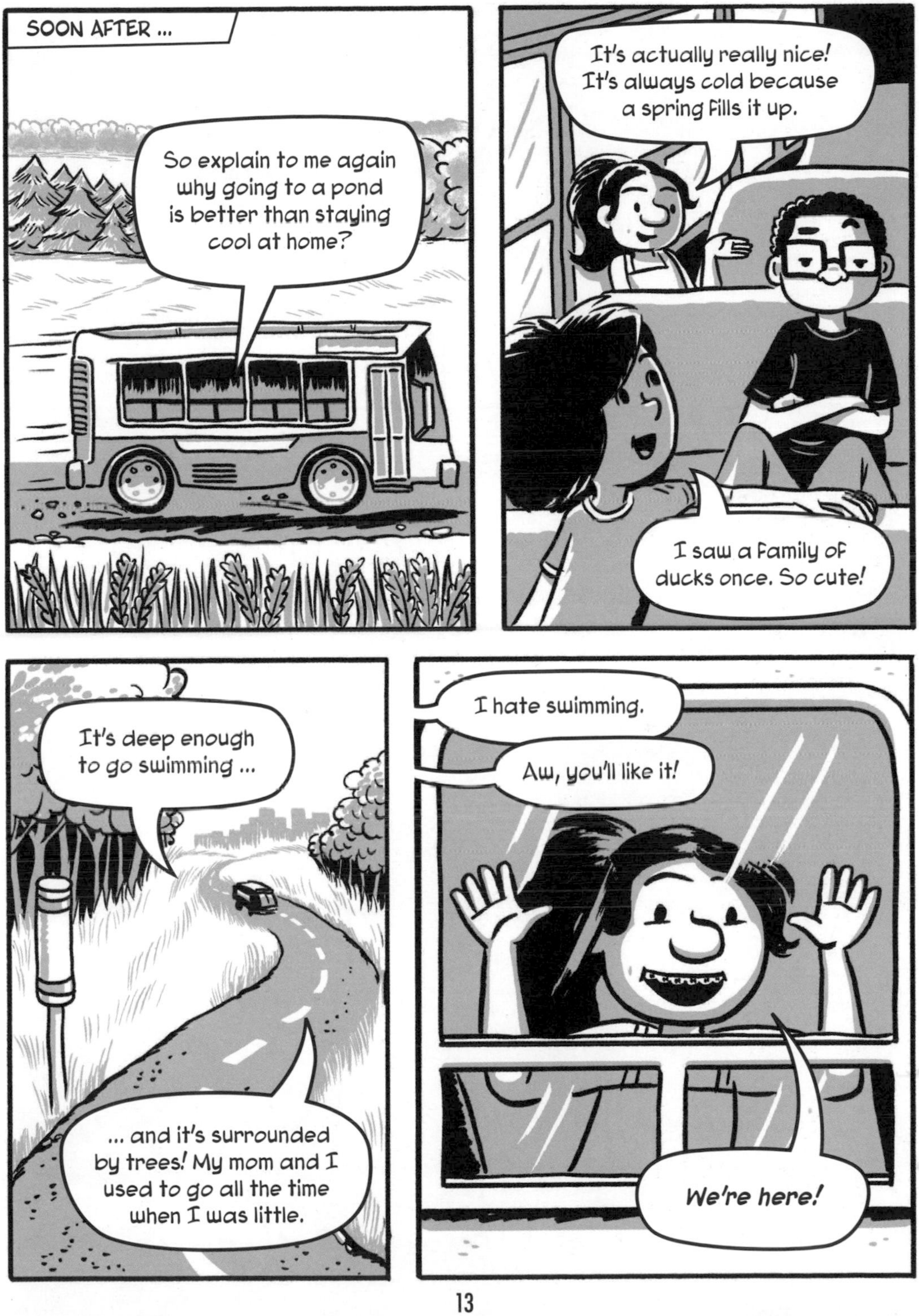
SOON AFTER ...
So explain to me again why going to a pond is better than staying cool at home?
It's actually really nice! It's always cold because a spring fills it up.
I saw a family of ducks once. So cute!
It's deep enough to go swimming ...
... and it's surrounded by trees! My mom and I used to go all the time when I was little.
I hate swimming.
Aw, you'll like it!
We're here!

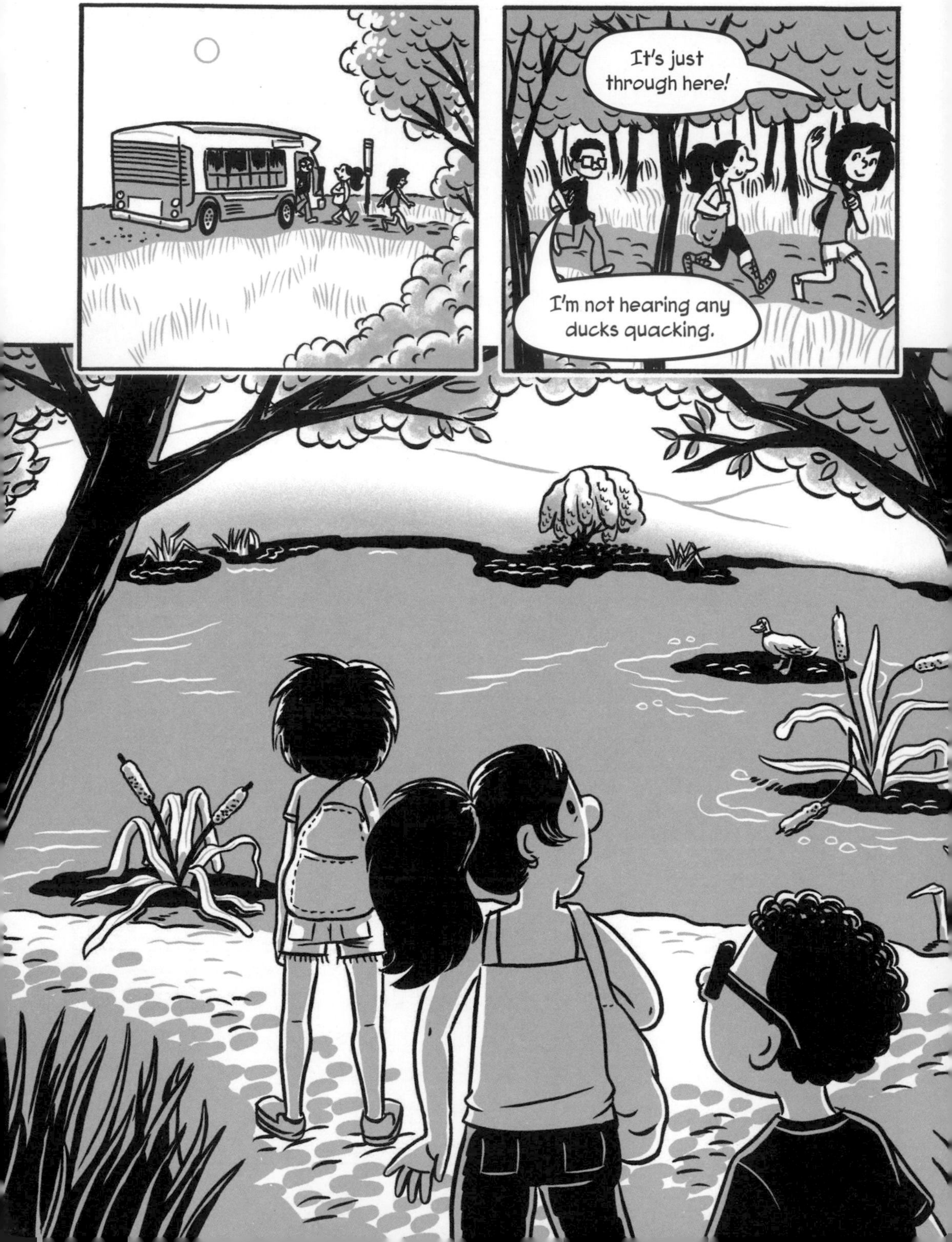
It's just through here!
I'm not hearing any ducks quacking.

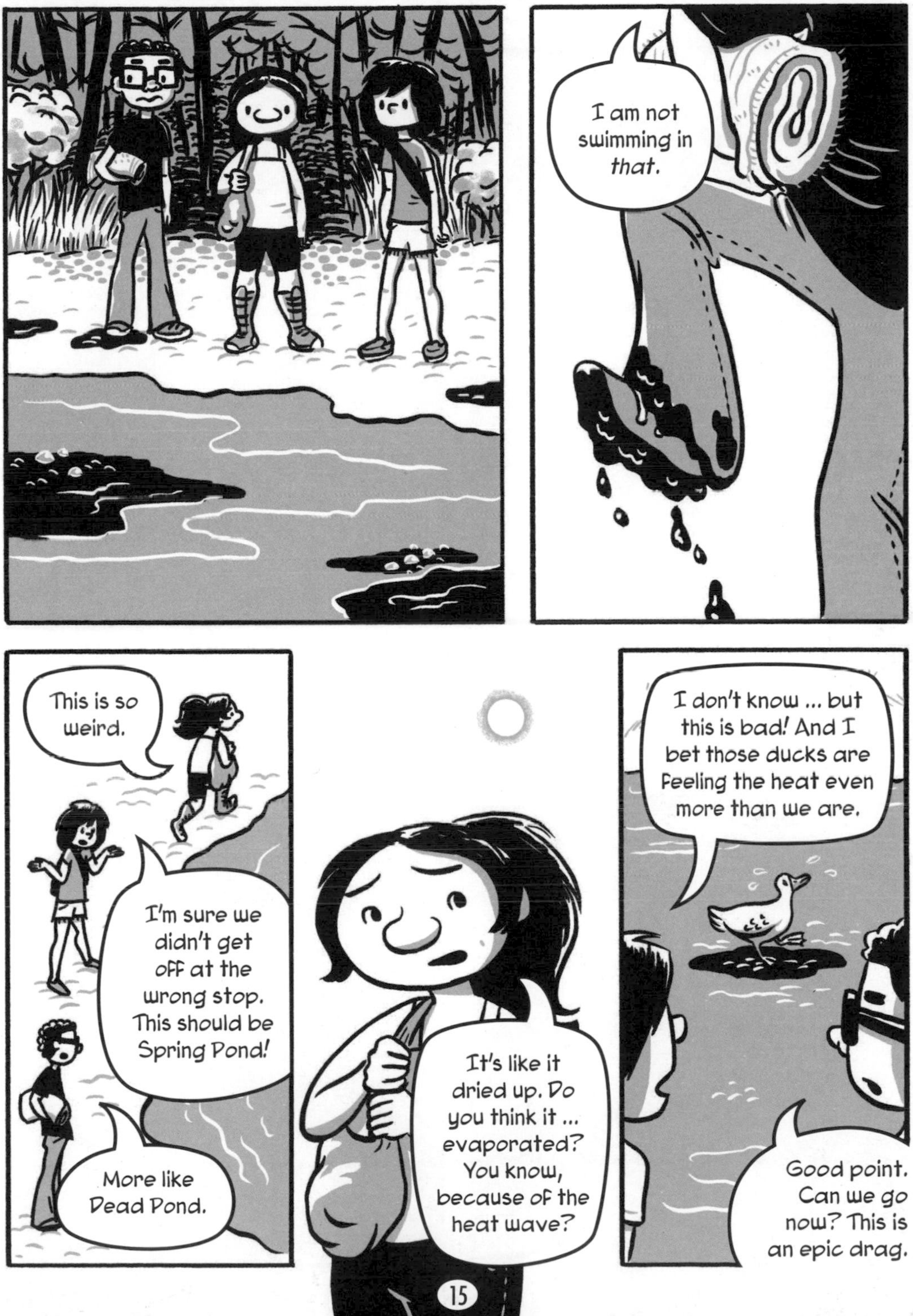
I am not swimming in *that*.
This is so weird.
I'm sure we didn't get off at the wrong stop. This should be Spring Pond!
More like Dead Pond.
It's like it dried up. Do you think it ... evaporated? You know, because of the heat wave?
I don't know ... but this is bad! And I bet those ducks are feeling the heat even more than we are.
Good point. Can we go now? This is an epic drag.

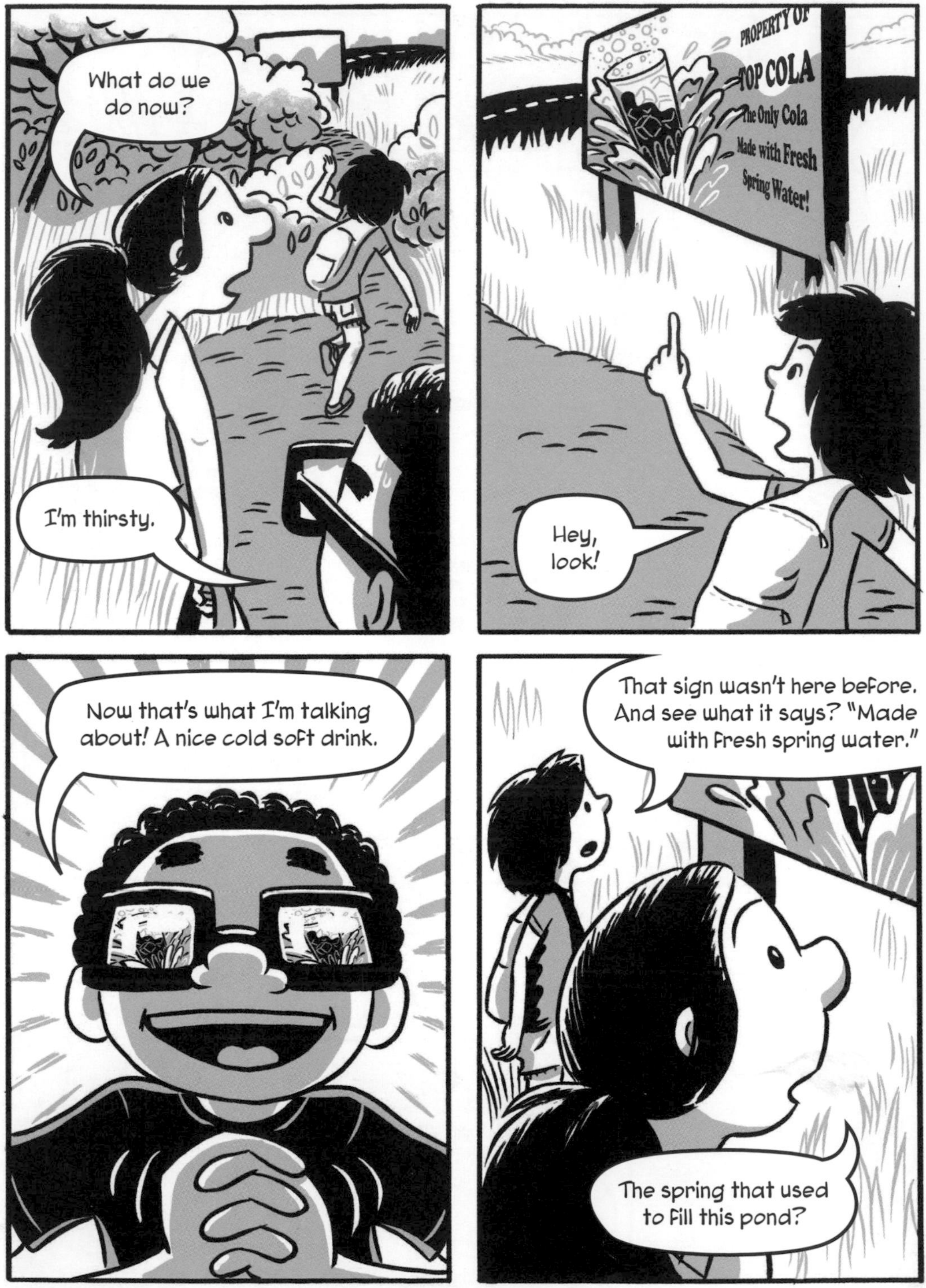
What do we do now?
I'm thirsty.
PROPERTY OF TOP COLA The Only Cola Made with Fresh Spring Water!
Hey, look!
Now that's what I'm talking about! A nice cold soft drink.
That sign wasn't here before. And see what it says? "Made with fresh spring water."
The spring that used to fill this pond?

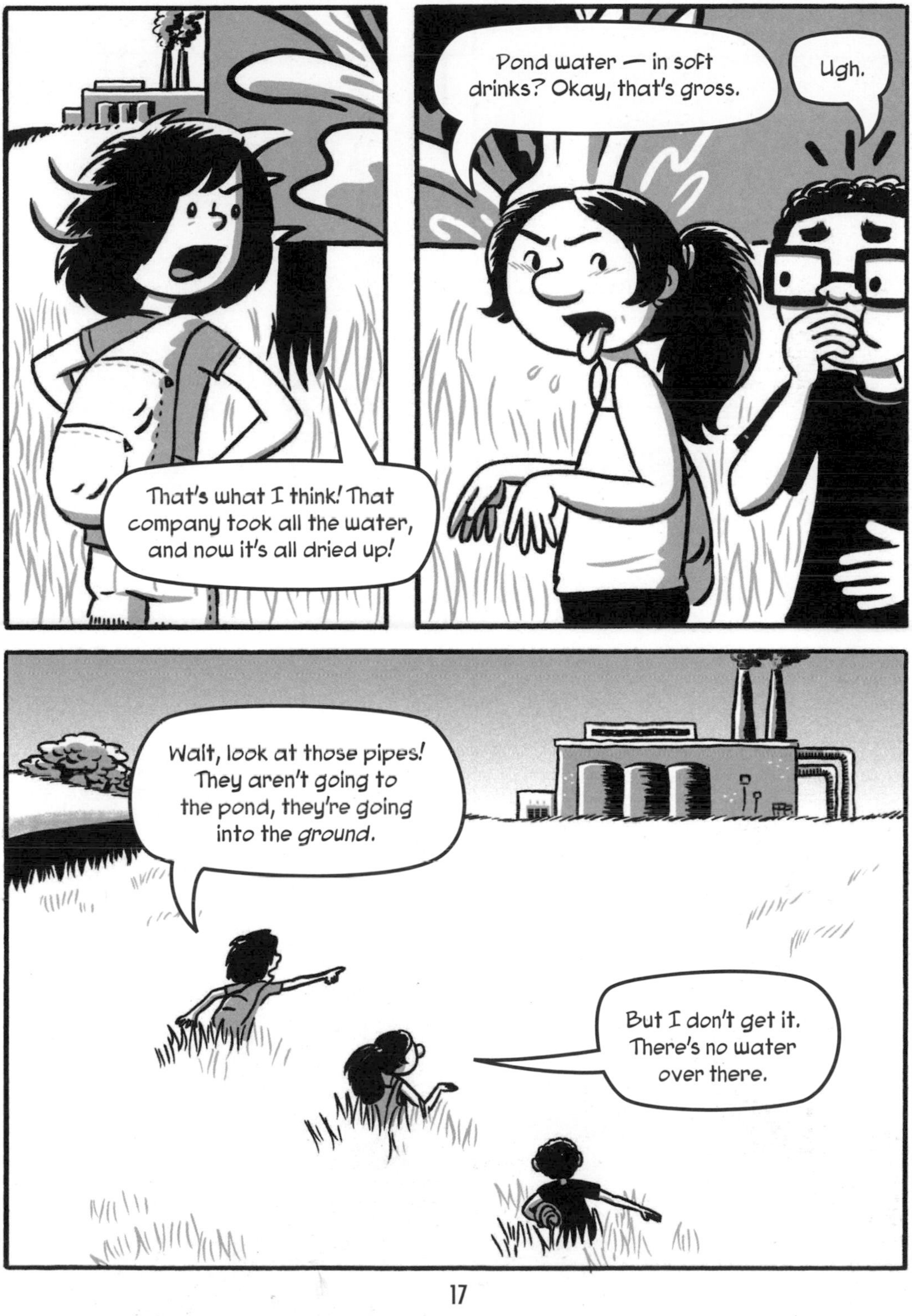
That's what I think! That company took all the water, and now it's all dried up!
Pond water — in soft drinks? Okay, that's gross.
Ugh.
Walt, look at those pipes! They aren't going to the pond, they're going into the *ground*.
But I don't get it. There's no water over there.

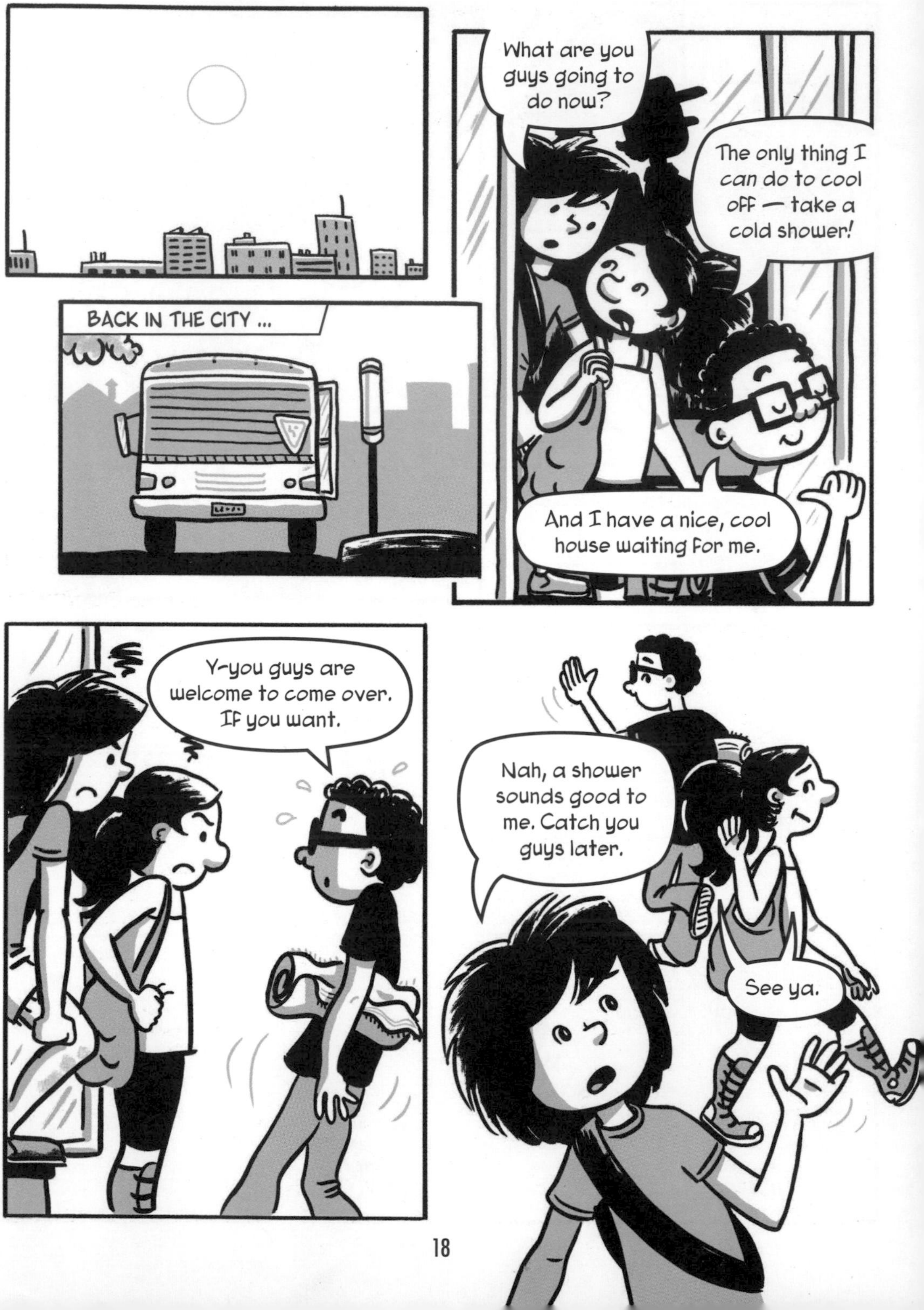
BACK IN THE CITY ...
What are you guys going to do now?
The only thing I can do to cool off — take a cold shower!
And I have a nice, cool house waiting for me.
Y-you guys are welcome to come over. If you want.
Nah, a shower sounds good to me. Catch you guys later.
See ya.

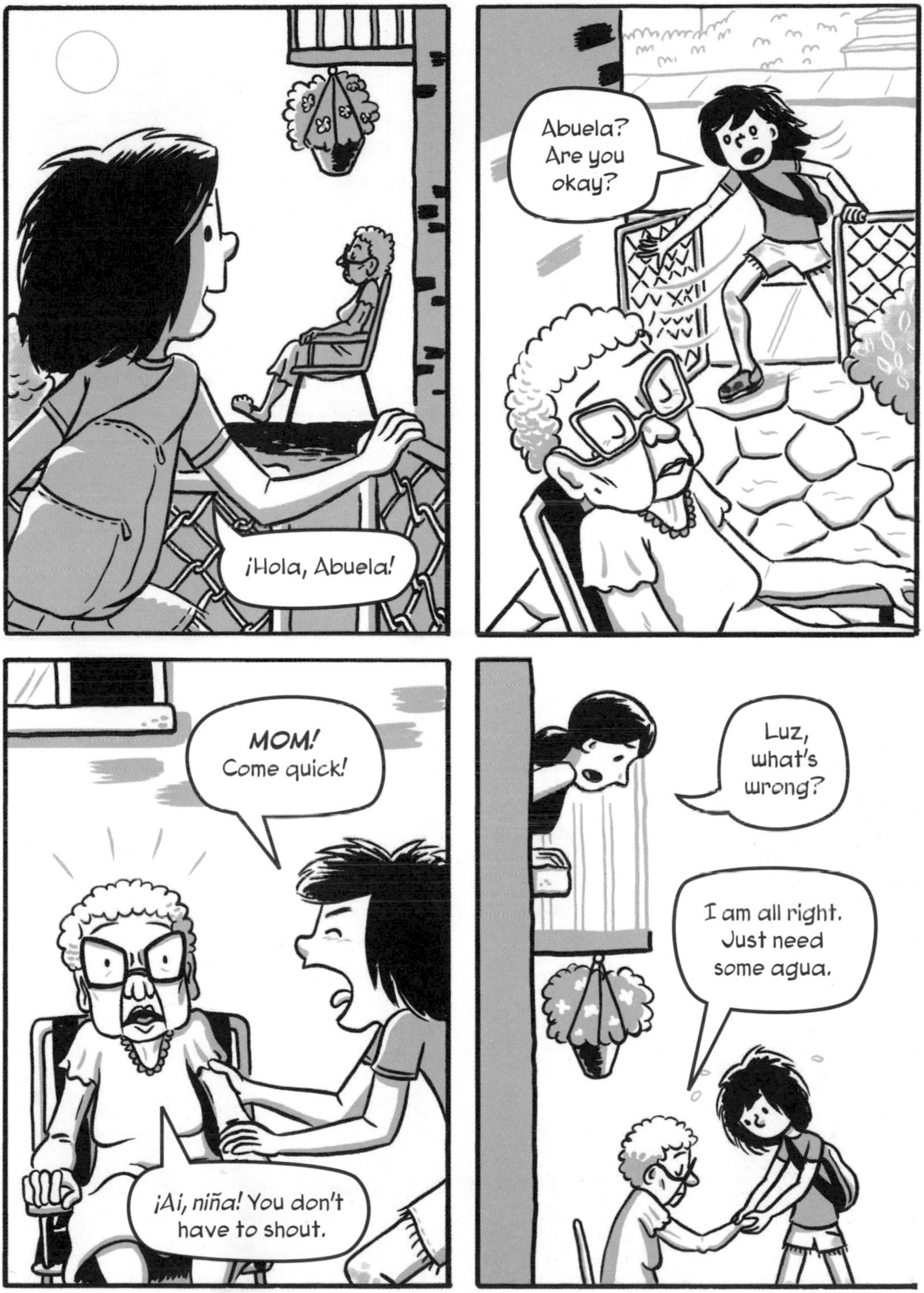
¡Hola, Abuela!
Abuela? Are you okay?
MOM! Come quick!
¡Ai, niña! You don't have to shout.
Luz, what's wrong?
I am all right. Just need some agua.

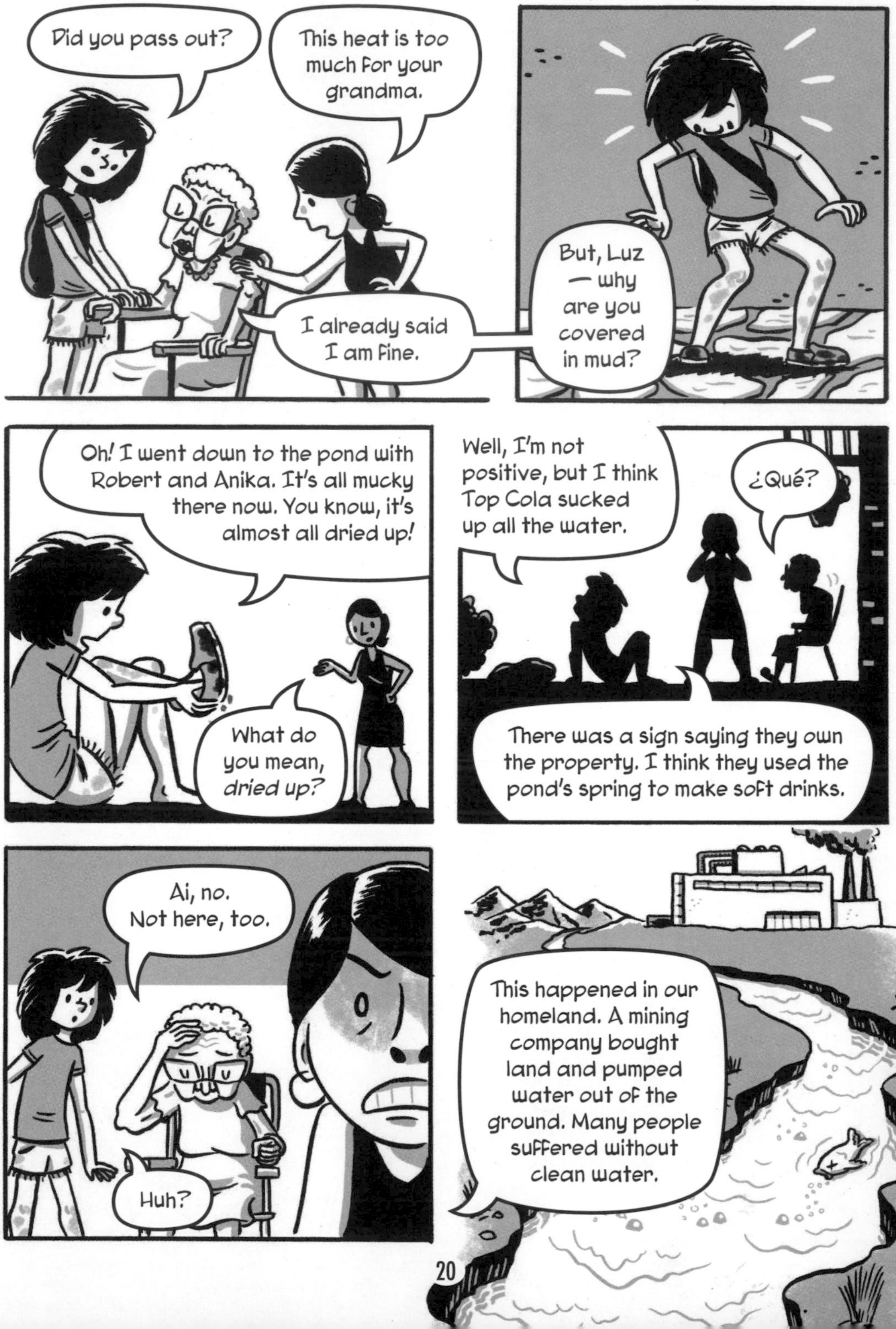

Did you pass out?
This heat is too much for your grandma.
I already said I am fine.
But, Luz — why are you covered in mud?
Oh! I went down to the pond with Robert and Anika. It's all mucky there now. You know, it's almost all dried up!
What do you mean, *dried up?*
Well, I'm not positive, but I think Top Cola sucked up all the water.
¿Qué?
There was a sign saying they own the property. I think they used the pond's spring to make soft drinks.
Ai, no. Not here, too.
Huh?
This happened in our homeland. A mining company bought land and pumped water out of the ground. Many people suffered without clean water.

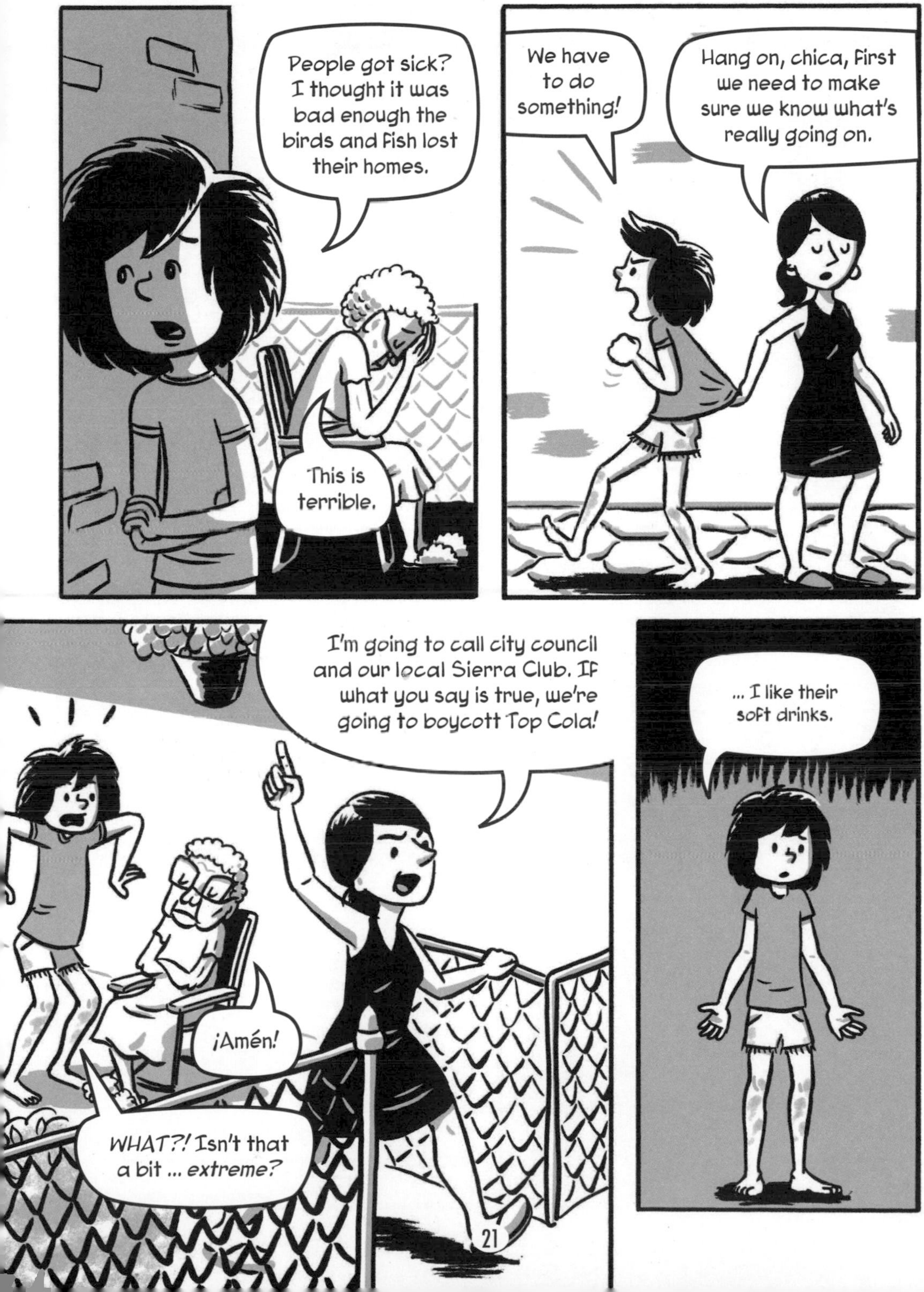
People got sick? I thought it was bad enough the birds and fish lost their homes.
This is terrible.
We have to do something!
Hang on, chica, first we need to make sure we know what's really going on.
I'm going to call city council and our local Sierra Club. If what you say is true, we're going to boycott Top Cola!
¡Amén!
WHAT?! Isn't that a bit ... *extreme?*
... I like their soft drinks.

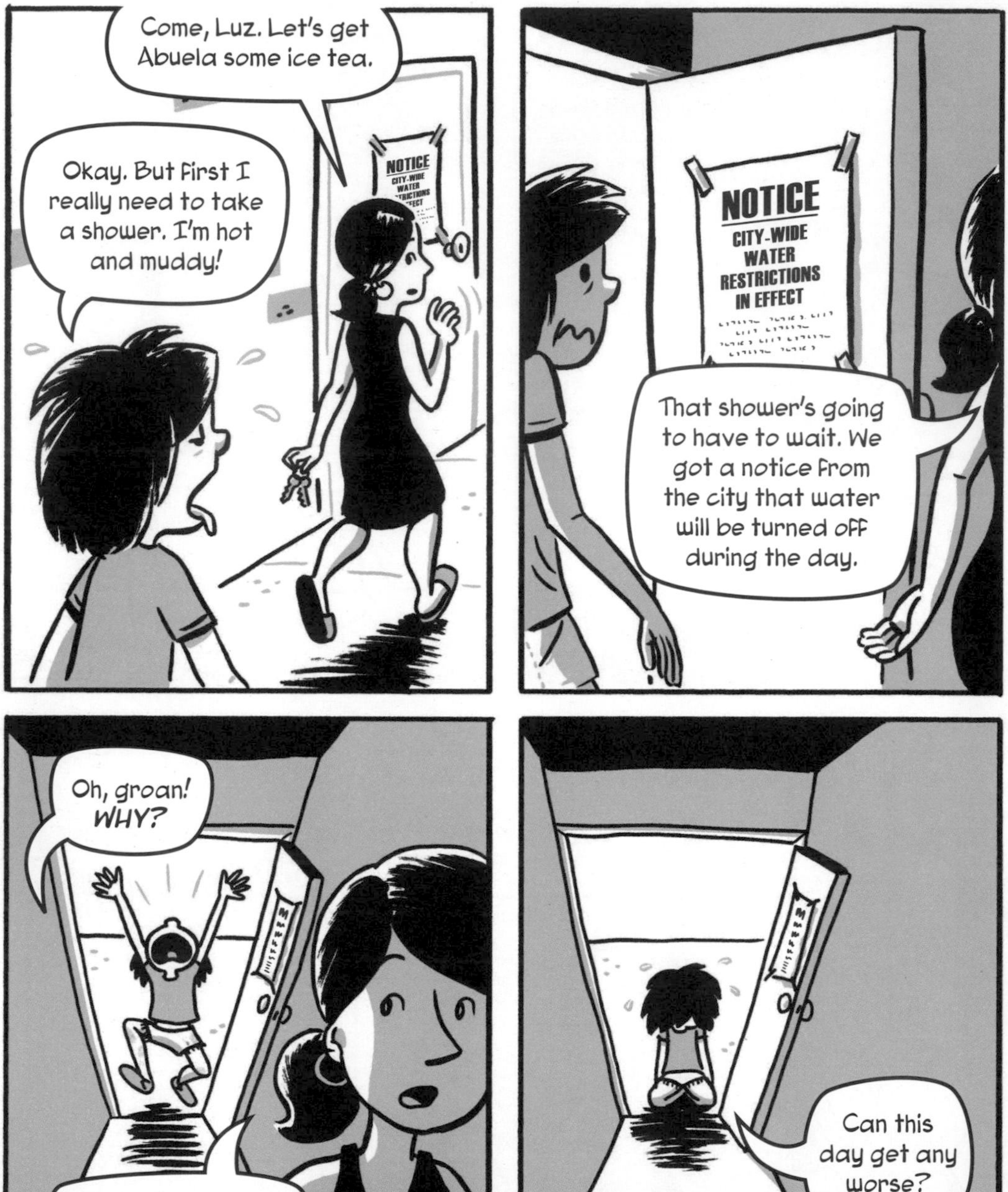
Come, Luz. Let's get Abuela some ice tea.
Okay. But first I really need to take a shower. I'm hot and muddy!
NOTICE
CITY-WIDE WATER RESTRICTIONS IN EFFECT
That shower's going to have to wait. We got a notice from the city that water will be turned off during the day.
Oh, groan! WHY?
To conserve water. I'm guessing it's because of this drought.
Can this day get any worse?

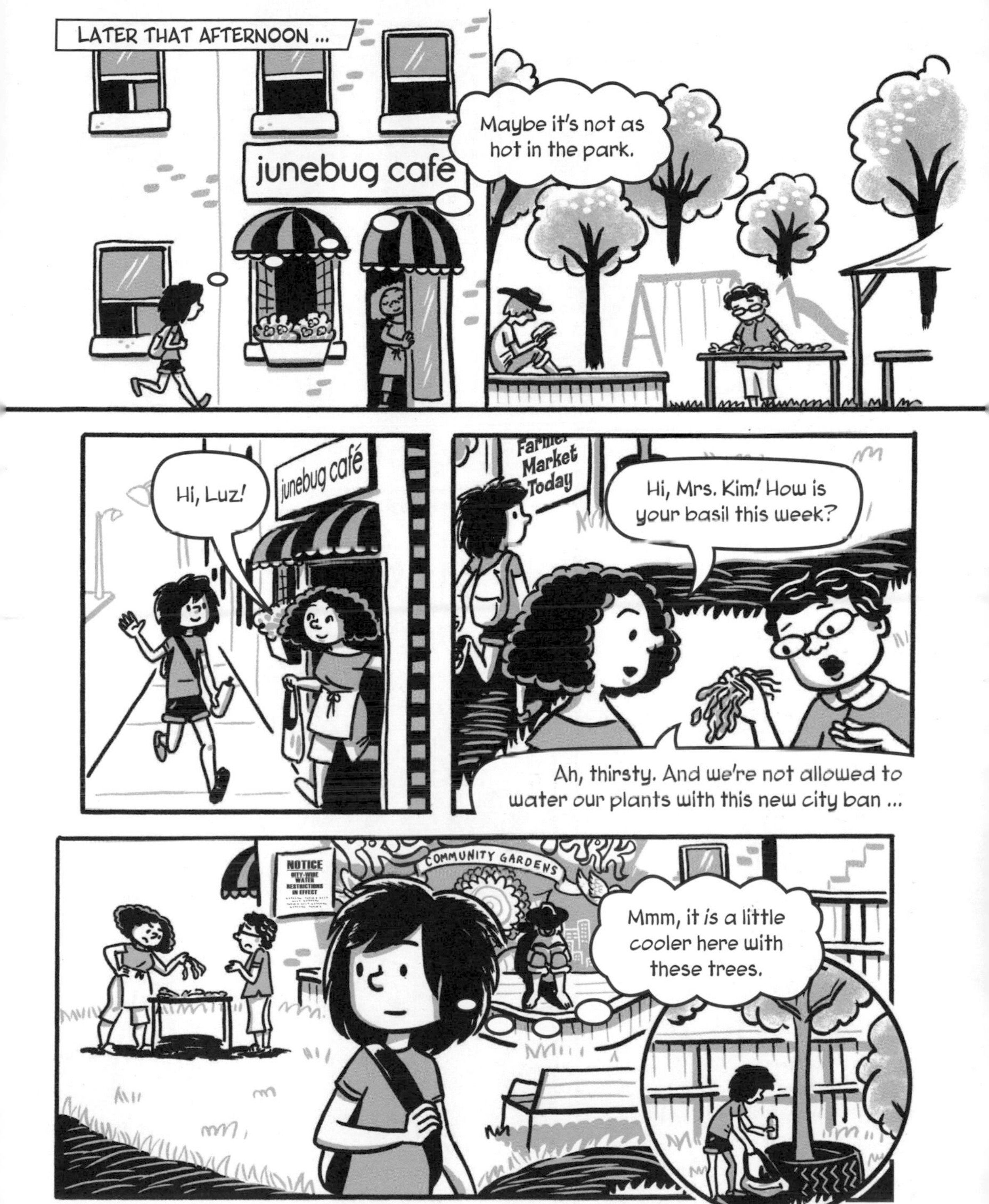
LATER THAT AFTERNOON ...
junebug café
Maybe it's not as hot in the park.
junebug café
Hi, Luz!
Farmer Market Today
Hi, Mrs. Kim! How is your basil this week?
Ah, thirsty. And we're not allowed to water our plants with this new city ban ...
NOTICE
CITY-WIDE WATER RESTRICTIONS IN EFFECT
COMMUNITY GARDENS
Mmm, it *is* a little cooler here with these trees.

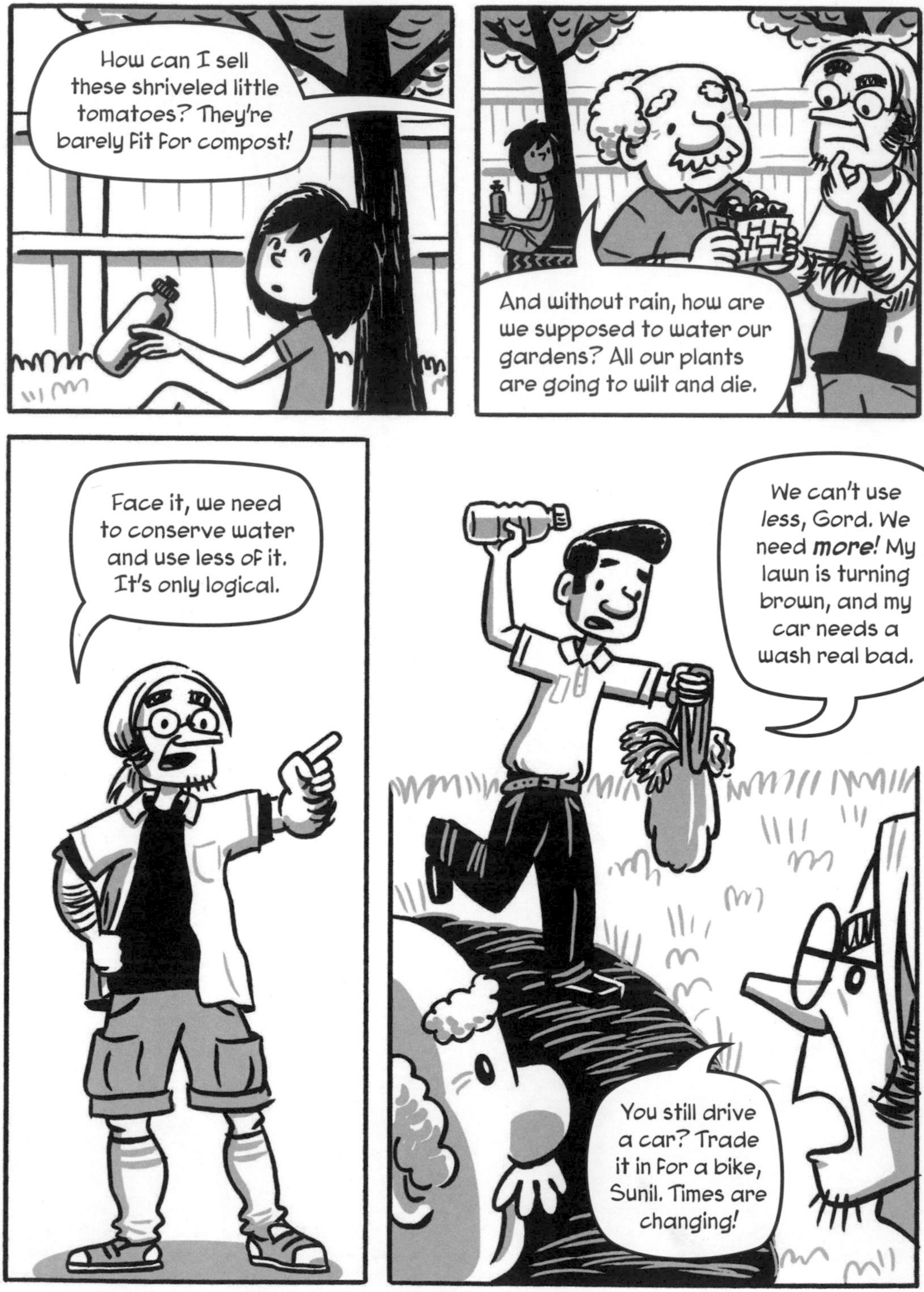
How can I sell these shriveled little tomatoes? They're barely fit for compost!
And without rain, how are we supposed to water our gardens? All our plants are going to wilt and die.
Face it, we need to conserve water and use less of it. It's only logical.
We can't use less, Gord. We need *more!* My lawn is turning brown, and my car needs a wash real bad.
You still drive a car? Trade it in for a bike, Sunil. Times are changing!

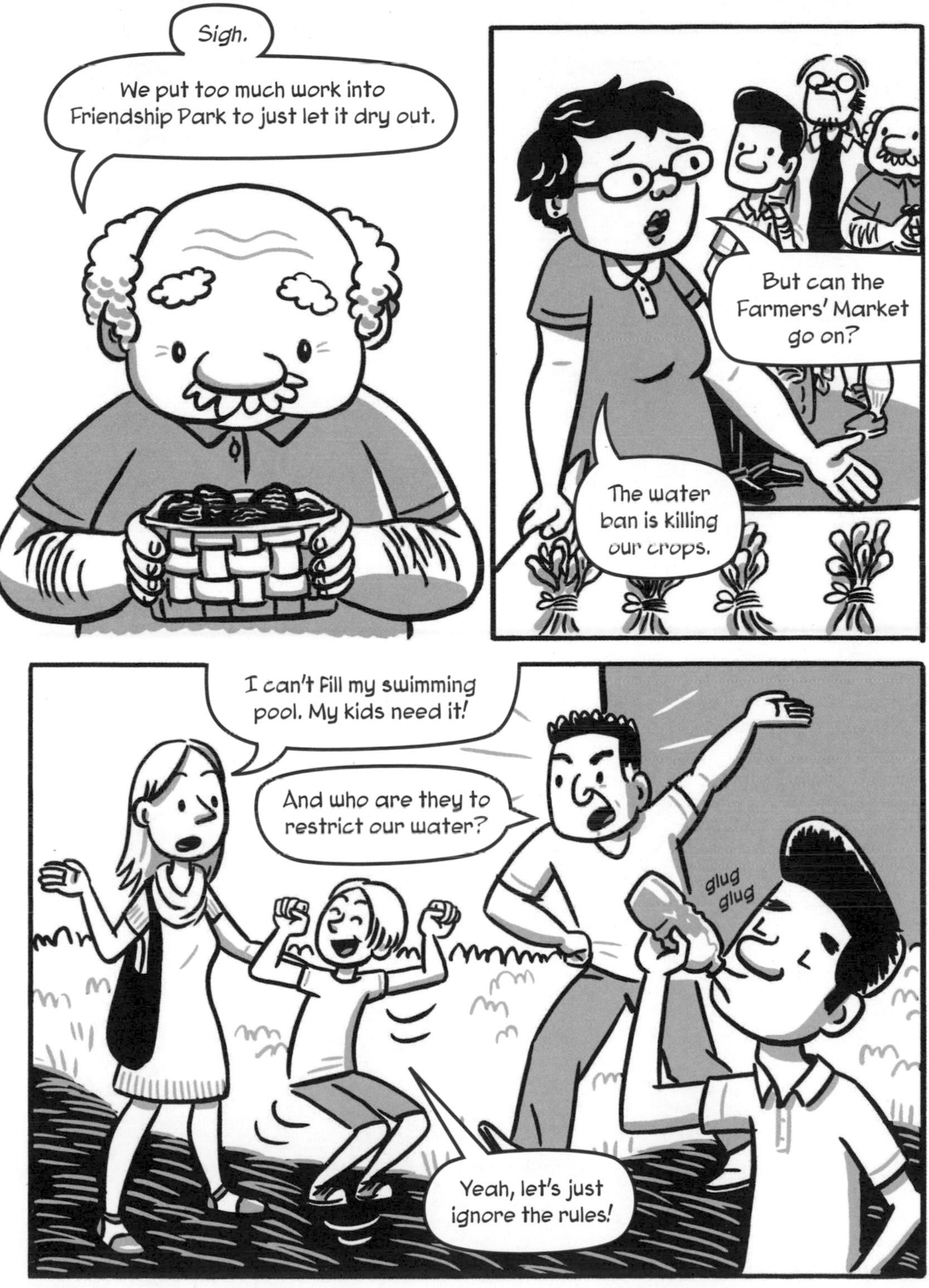
Sigh.
We put too much work into Friendship Park to just let it dry out.
But can the Farmers' Market go on?
The water ban is killing our crops.
I can't fill my swimming pool. My kids need it!
And who are they to restrict our water?
glug glug
Yeah, let's just ignore the rules!

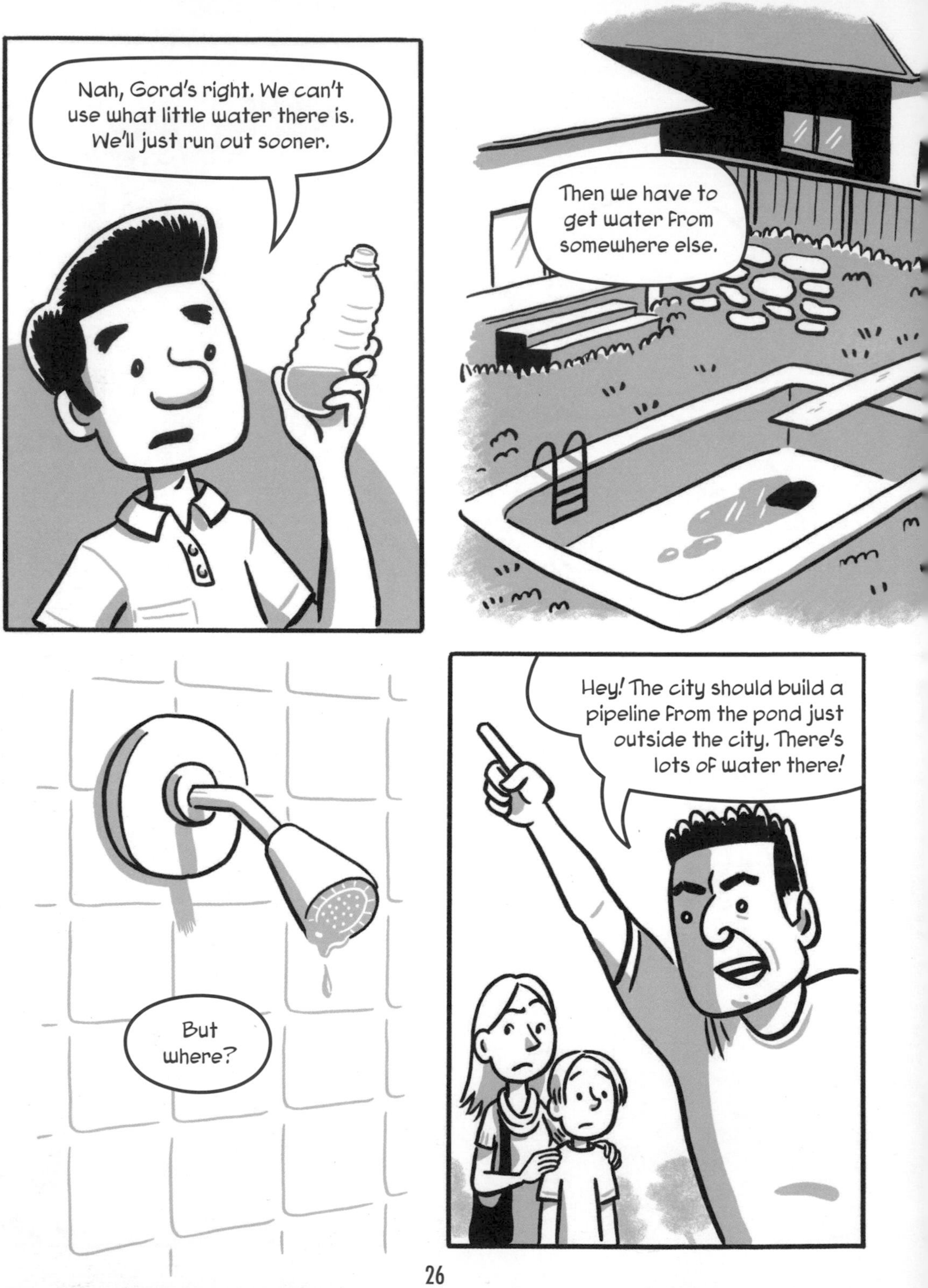
Nah, Gord's right. We can't use what little water there is. We'll just run out sooner.
Then we have to get water from somewhere else.
But where?
Hey! The city should build a pipeline from the pond just outside the city. There's lots of water there!

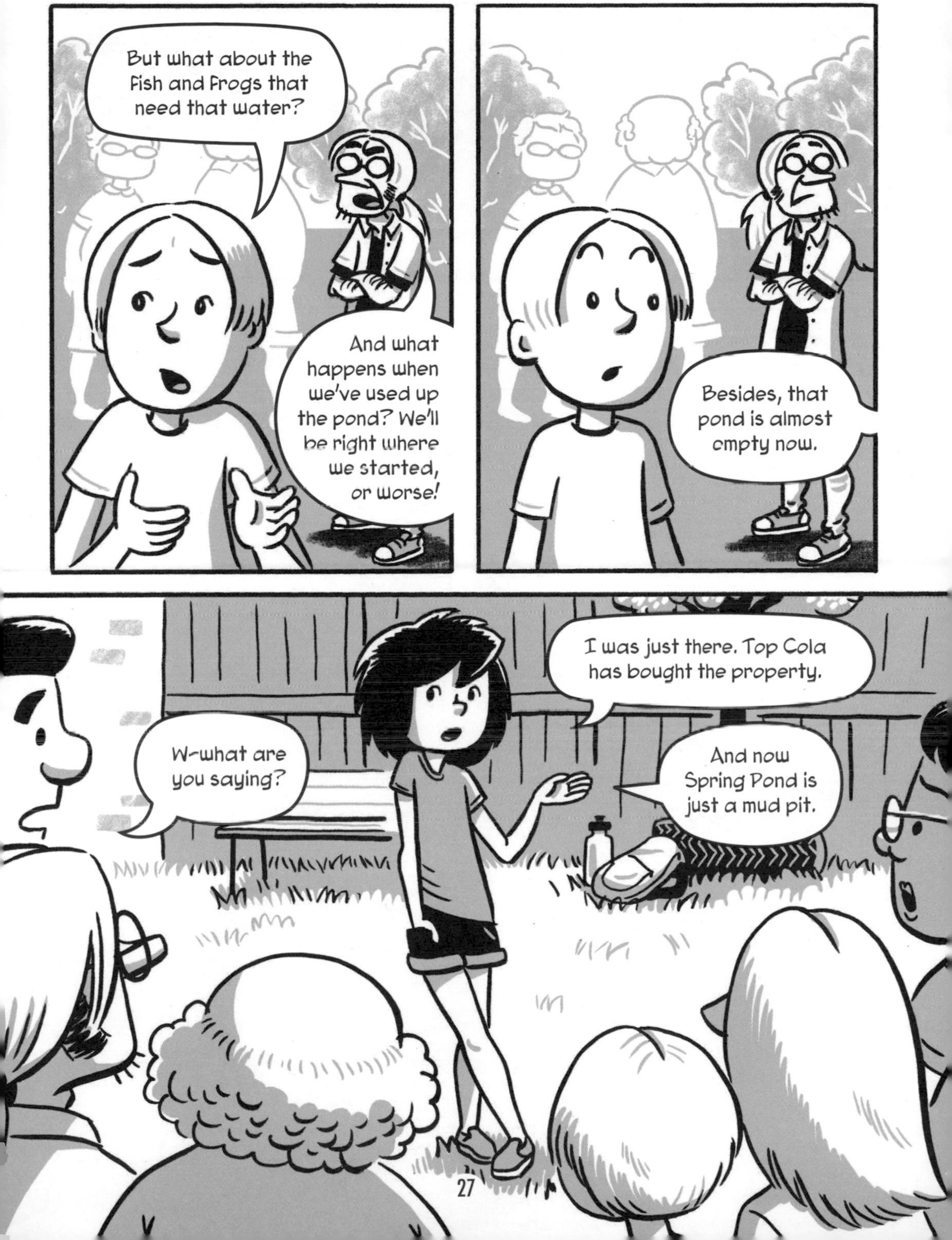
But what about the fish and frogs that need that water?
And what happens when we've used up the pond? We'll be right where we started, or worse!
Besides, that pond is almost empty now.
I was just there. Top Cola has bought the property.
W-what are you saying?
And now Spring Pond is just a mud pit.

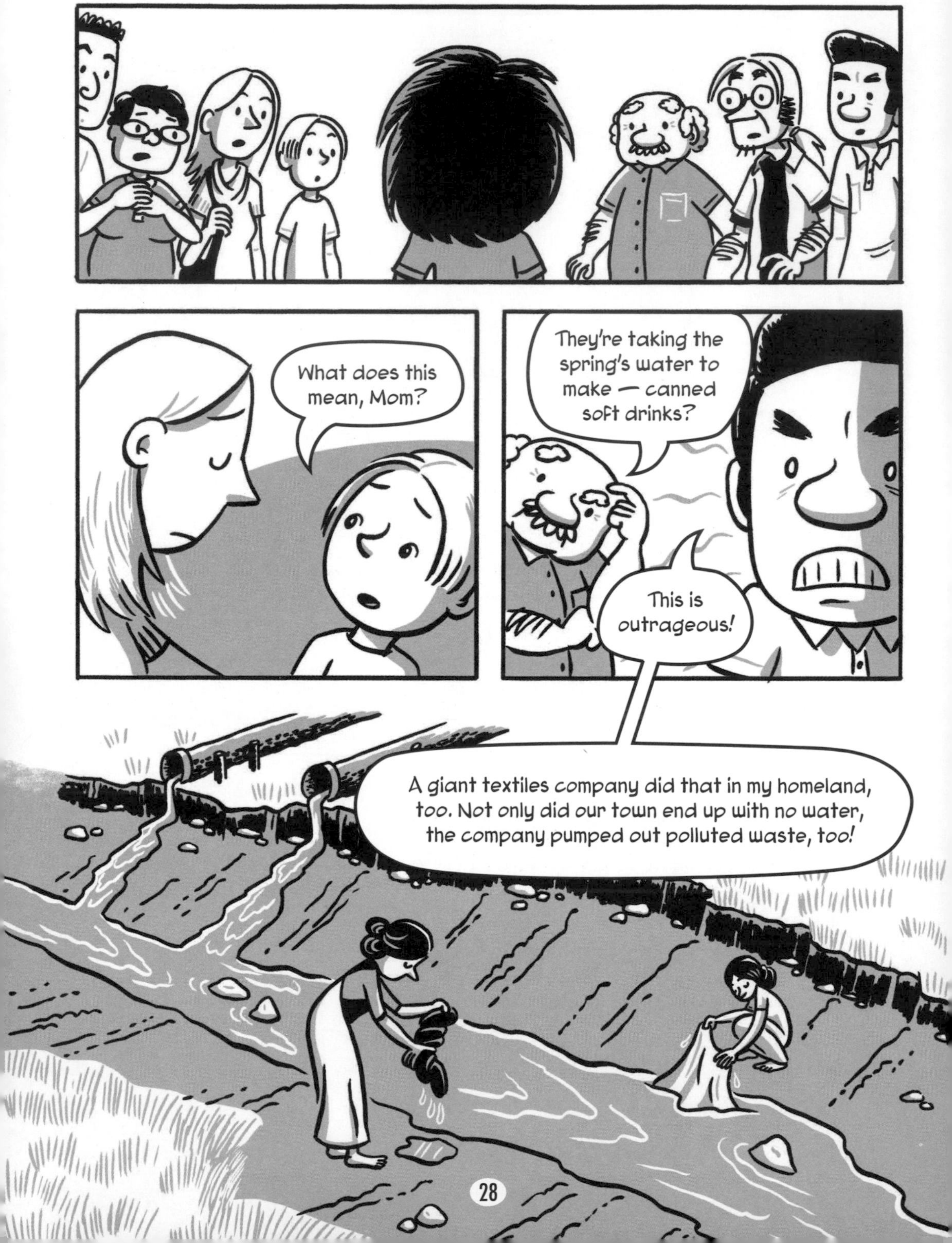
What does this mean, Mom?
They're taking the spring's water to make — canned soft drinks?
This is outrageous!
A giant textiles company did that in my homeland, too. Not only did our town end up with no water, the company pumped out polluted waste, too!

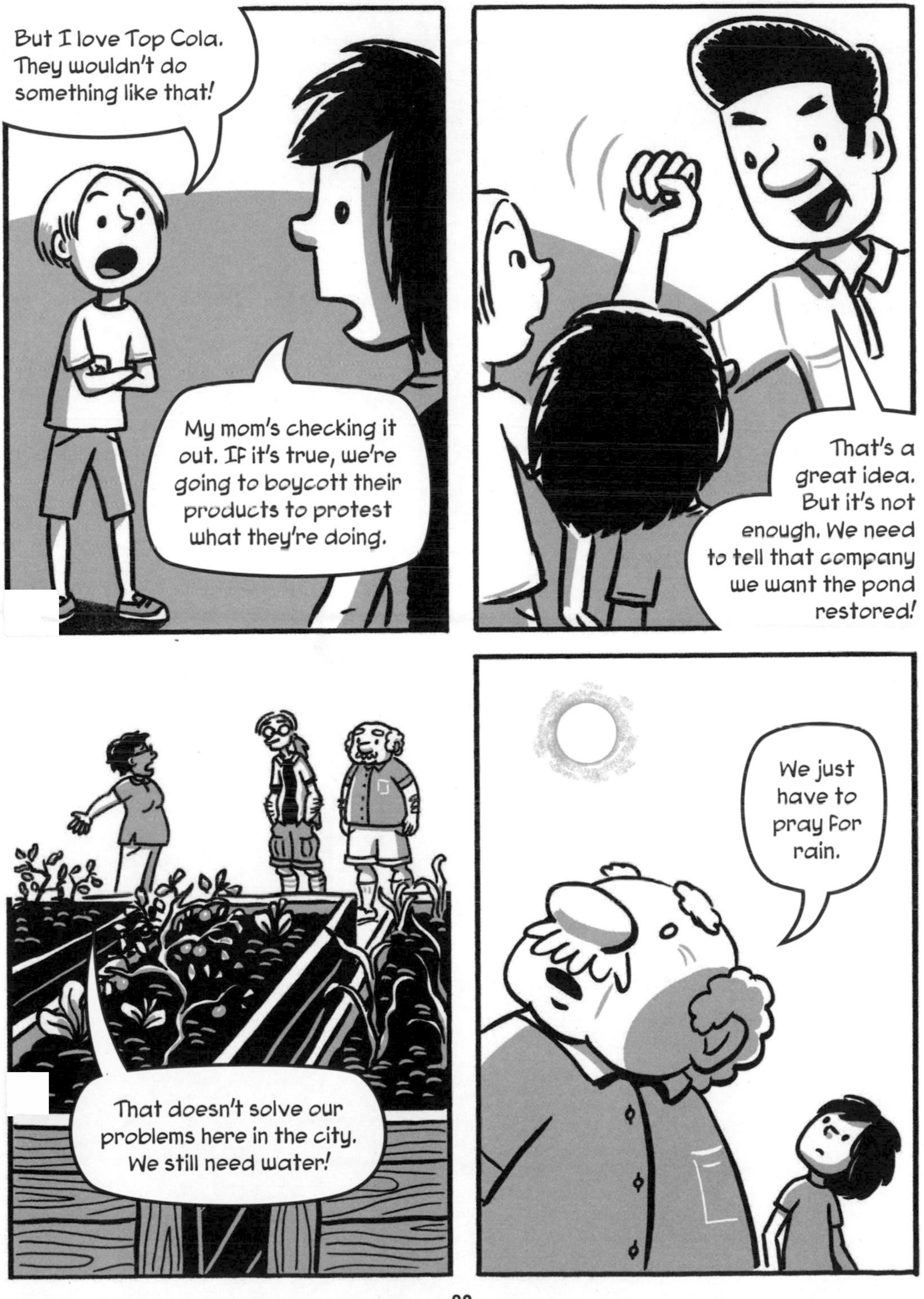
But I love Top Cola. They wouldn't do something like that!
My mom's checking it out. If it's true, we're going to boycott their products to protest what they're doing.
That's a great idea. But it's not enough. We need to tell that company we want the pond restored!
That doesn't solve our problems here in the city. We still need water!
We just have to pray for rain.

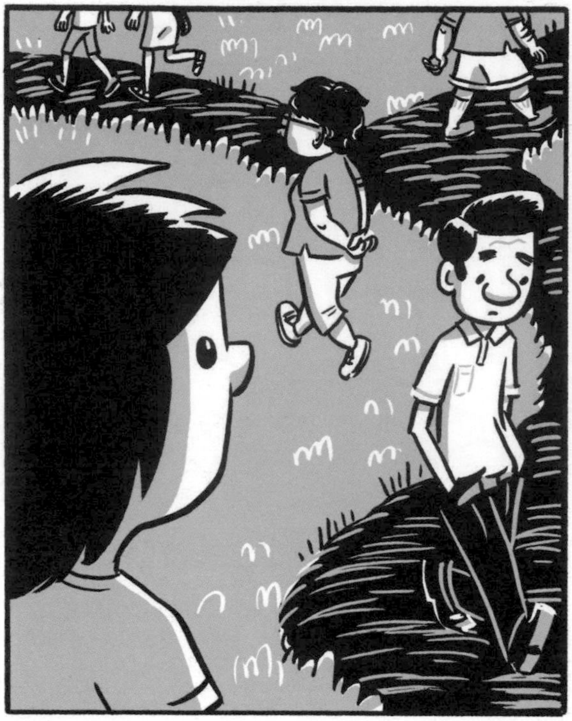

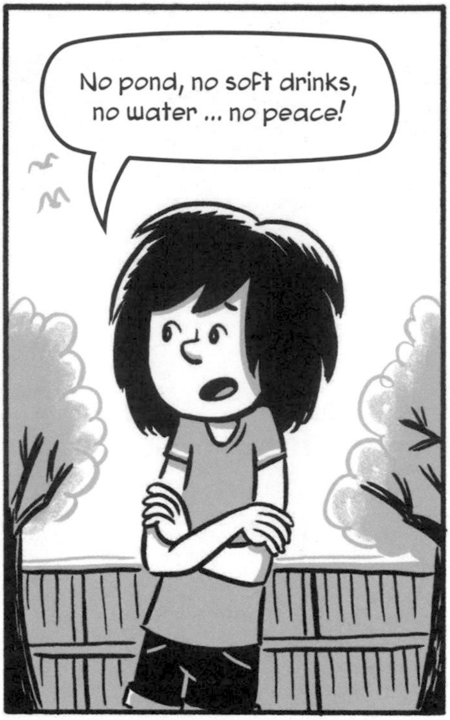
No pond, no soft drinks,
no water ... no peace!

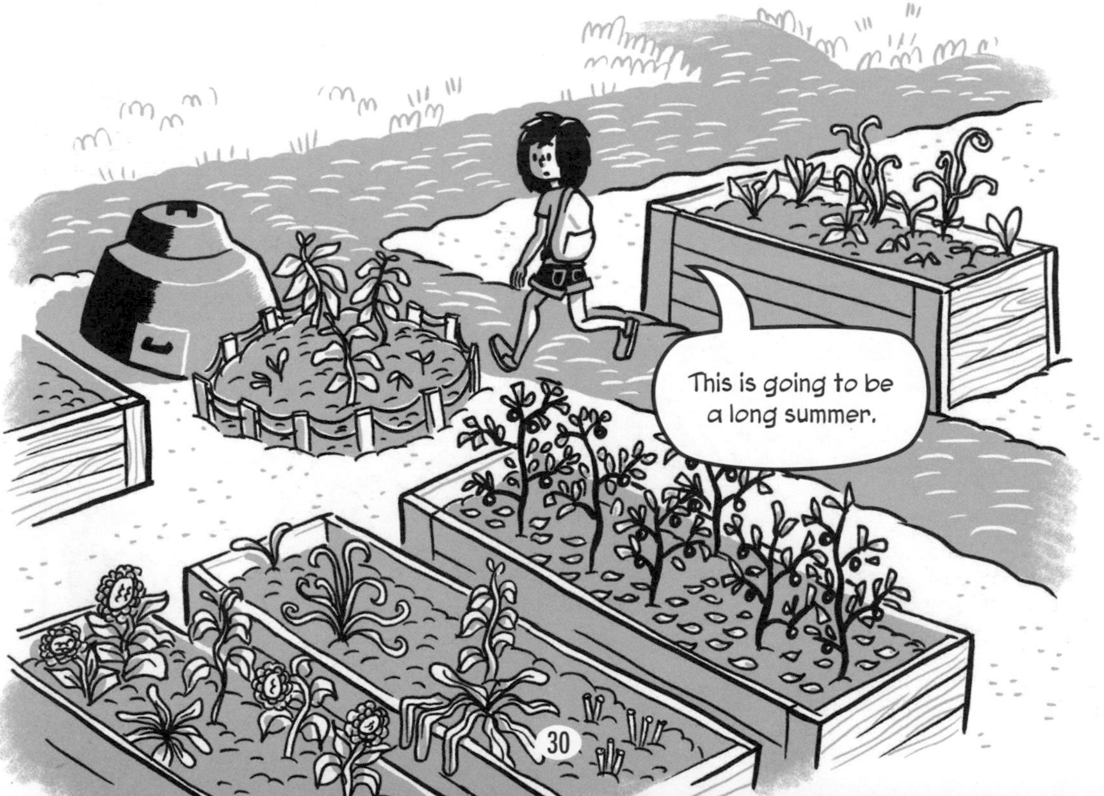
This is going to be
a long summer.

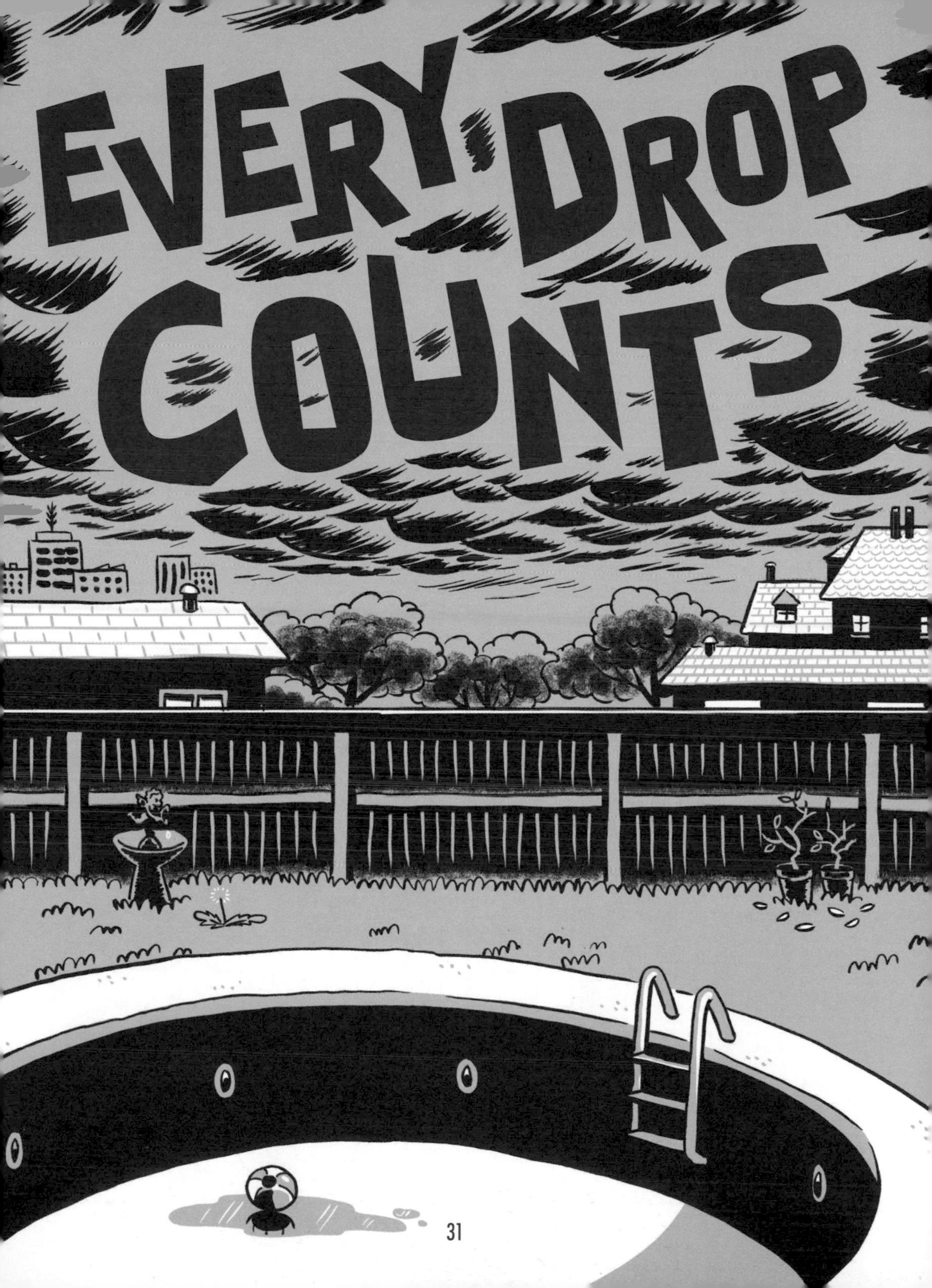
EVERY DROP COUNTS

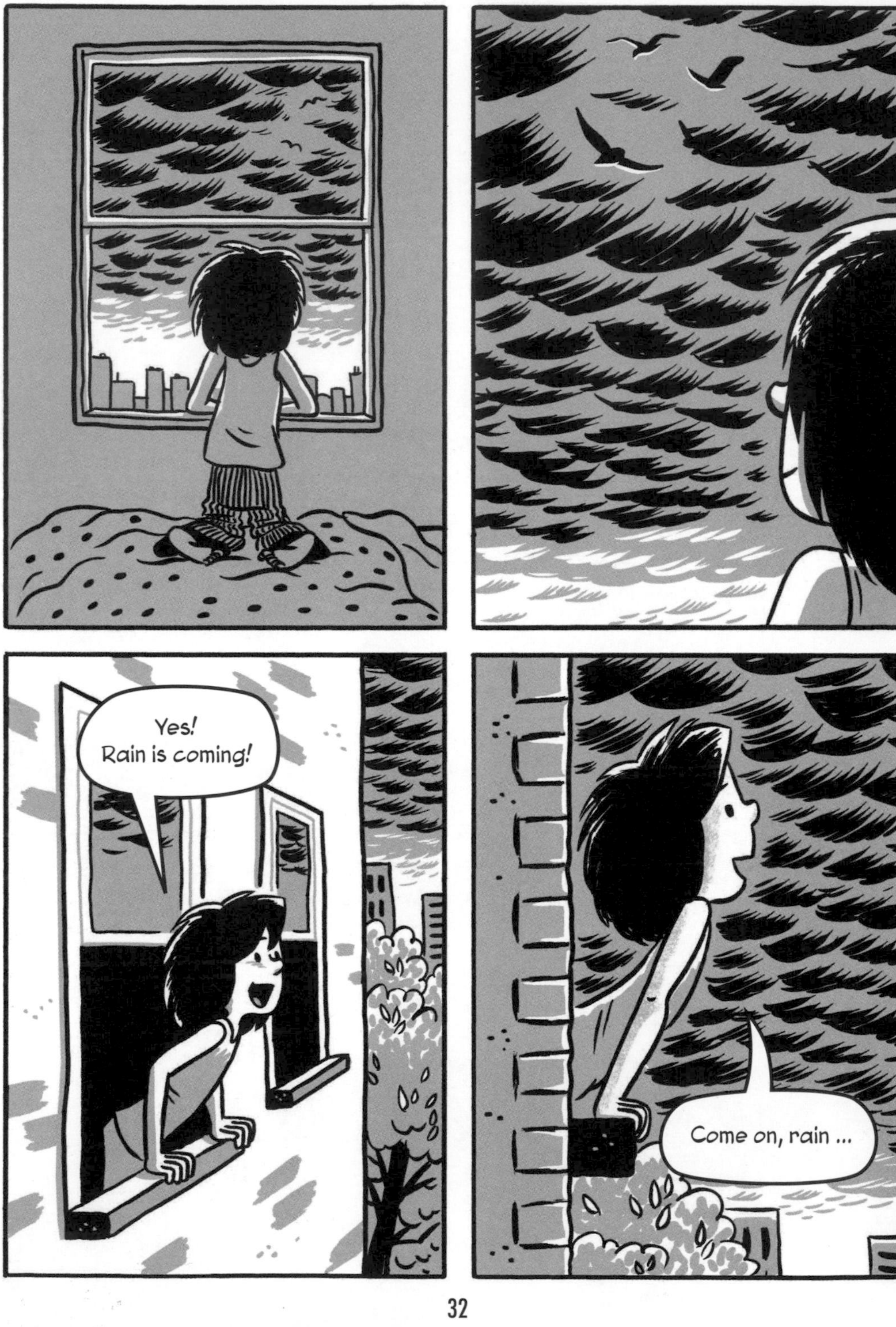
Yes! Rain is coming!
Come on, rain ...

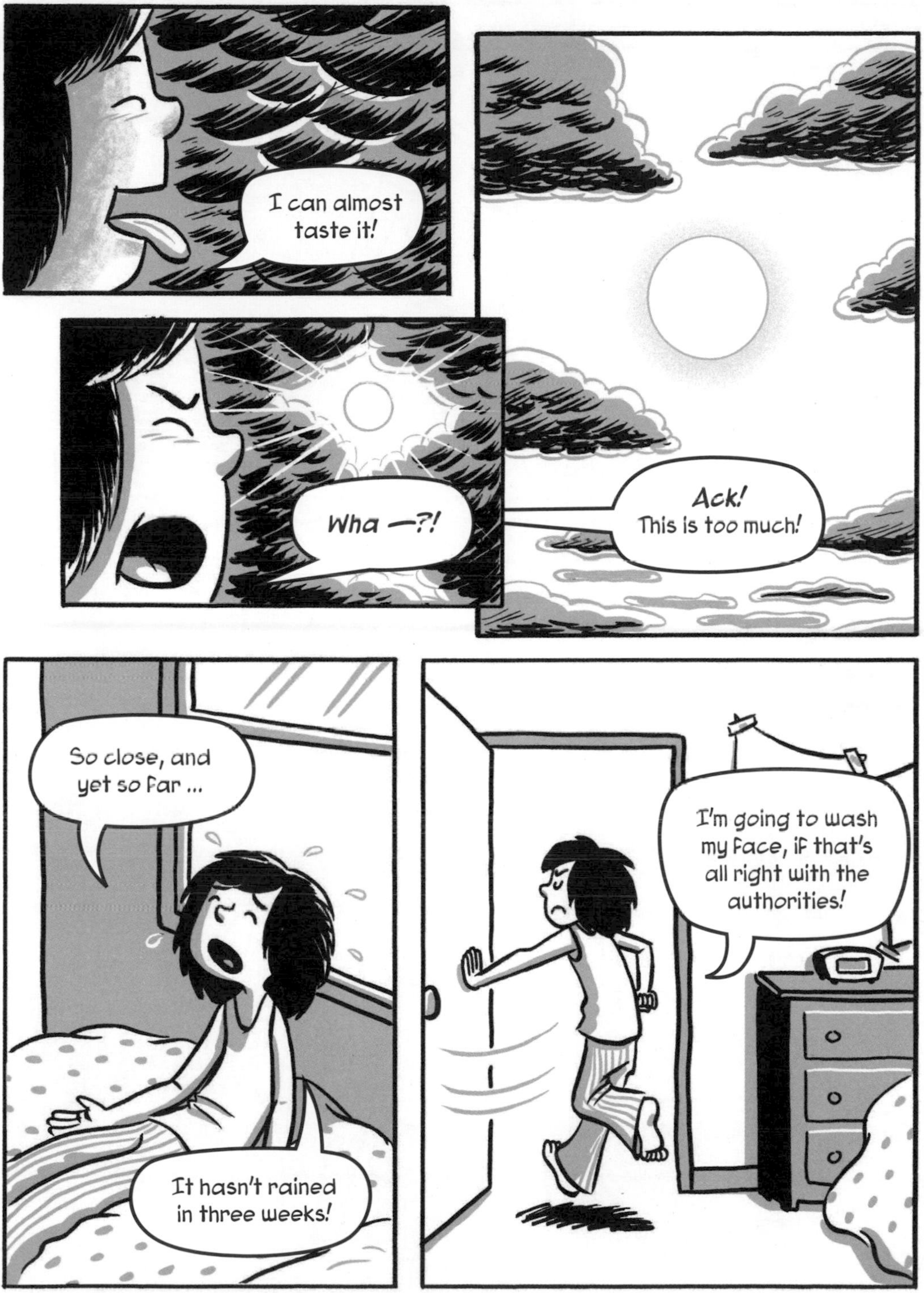
I can almost taste it!
Wha —?!
Ack! This is too much!
So close, and yet so far ...
It hasn't rained in three weeks!
I'm going to wash my face, if that's all right with the authorities!

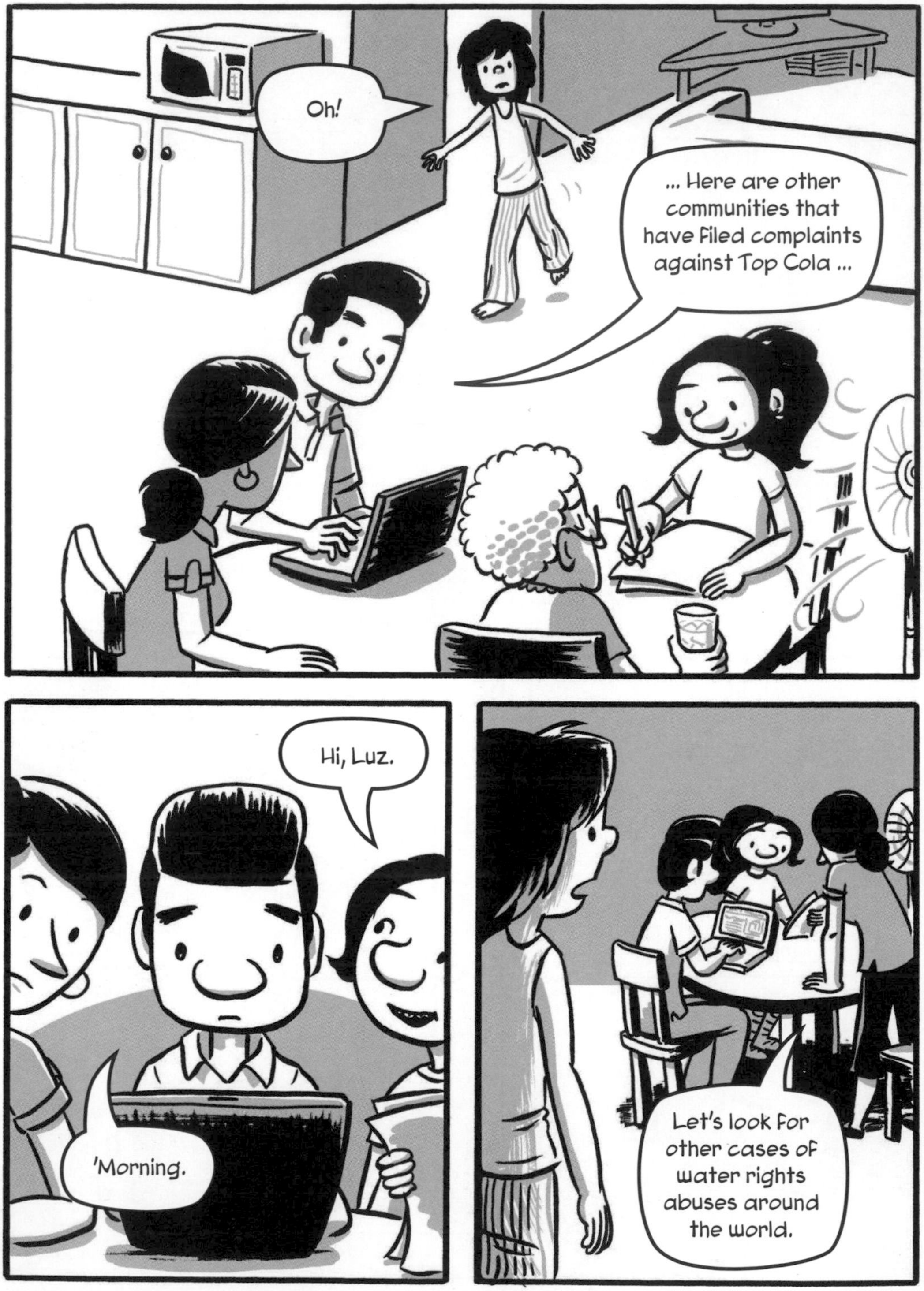
Oh!
... Here are other communities that have filed complaints against Top Cola ...
Hi, Luz.
'Morning.
Let's look for other cases of water rights abuses around the world.

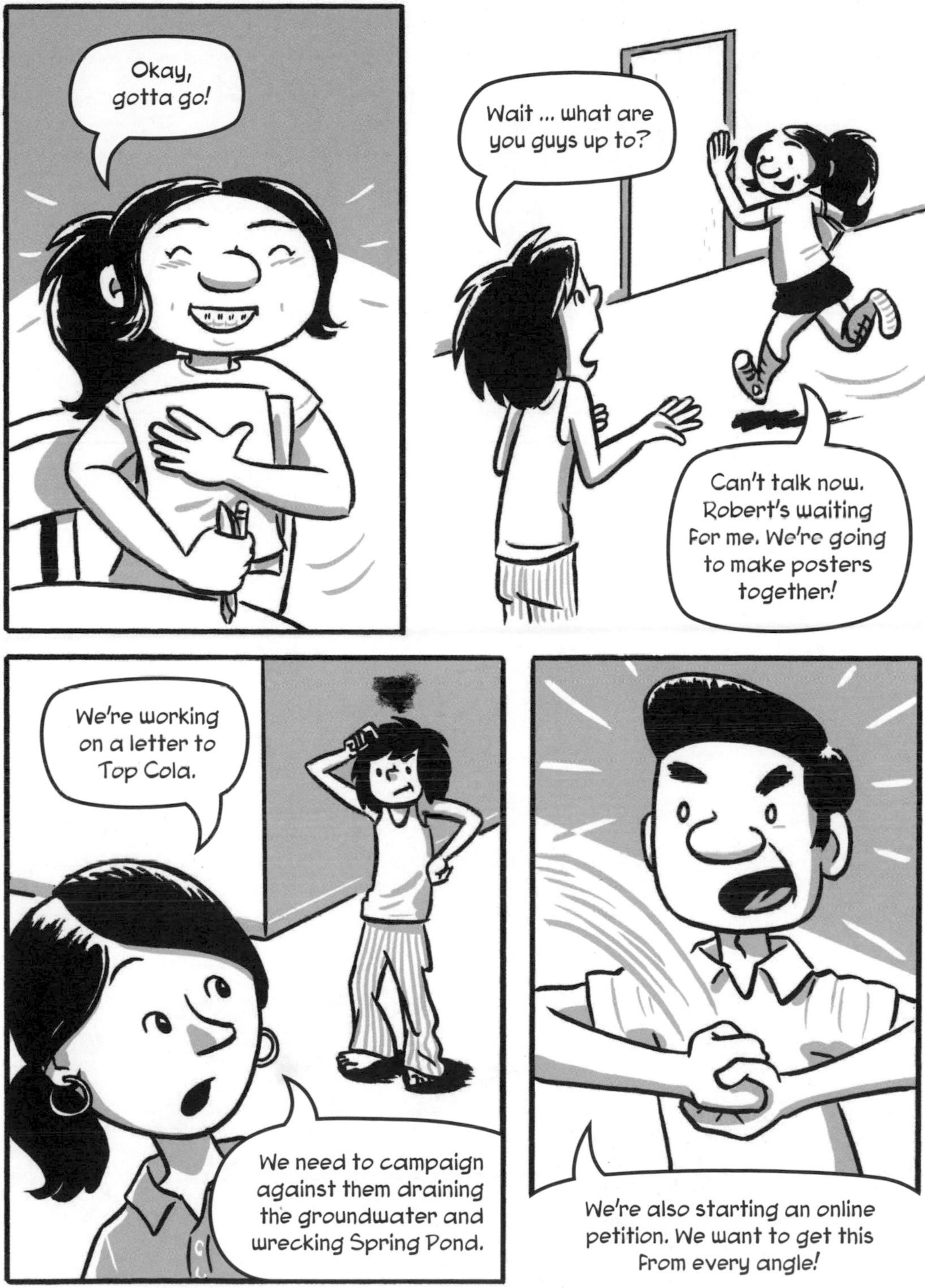
Okay, gotta go!
Wait ... what are you guys up to?
Can't talk now. Robert's waiting for me. We're going to make posters together!
We're working on a letter to Top Cola.
We need to campaign against them draining the groundwater and wrecking Spring Pond.
We're also starting an online petition. We want to get this from every angle!

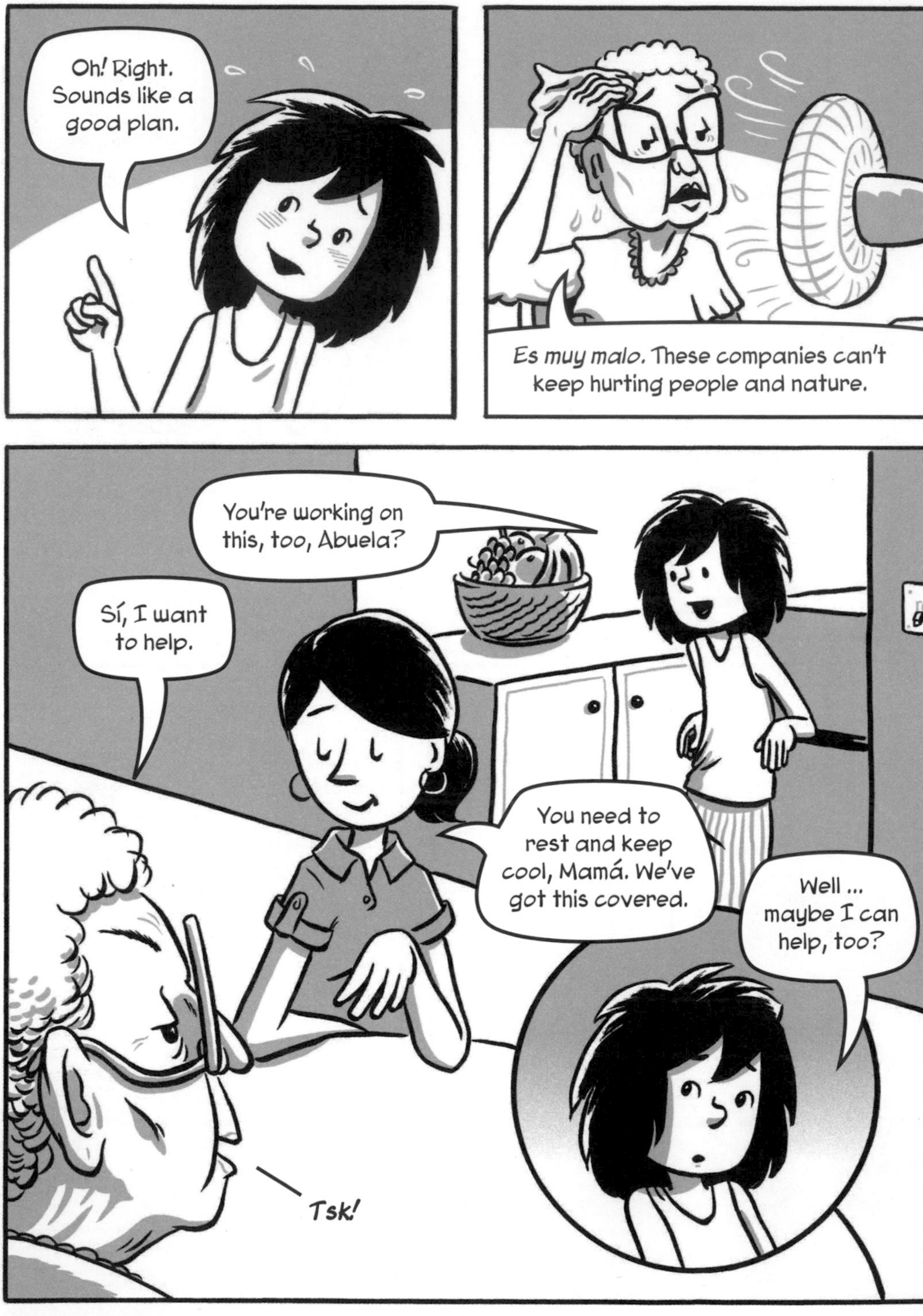
Oh! Right. Sounds like a good plan.
Es muy malo. These companies can't keep hurting people and nature.
You're working on this, too, Abuela?
Sí, I want to help.
You need to rest and keep cool, Mamá. We've got this covered.
Well ... maybe I can help, too?
Tsk!

38

39

41

In nature, there is always water deep underground. Rivers and streams trickle into the soil along with rainwater.

But in the city, there's very little groundwater — instead, we have basements and subways and sewers.

When it rains, water can't land on the soil because buildings and roads cover the ground! Rain is lost into sewer pipes.

It spreads all over, and plants can drink it up through their roots to keep healthy and growing.

So plants get watered by rain above, as well as from below!

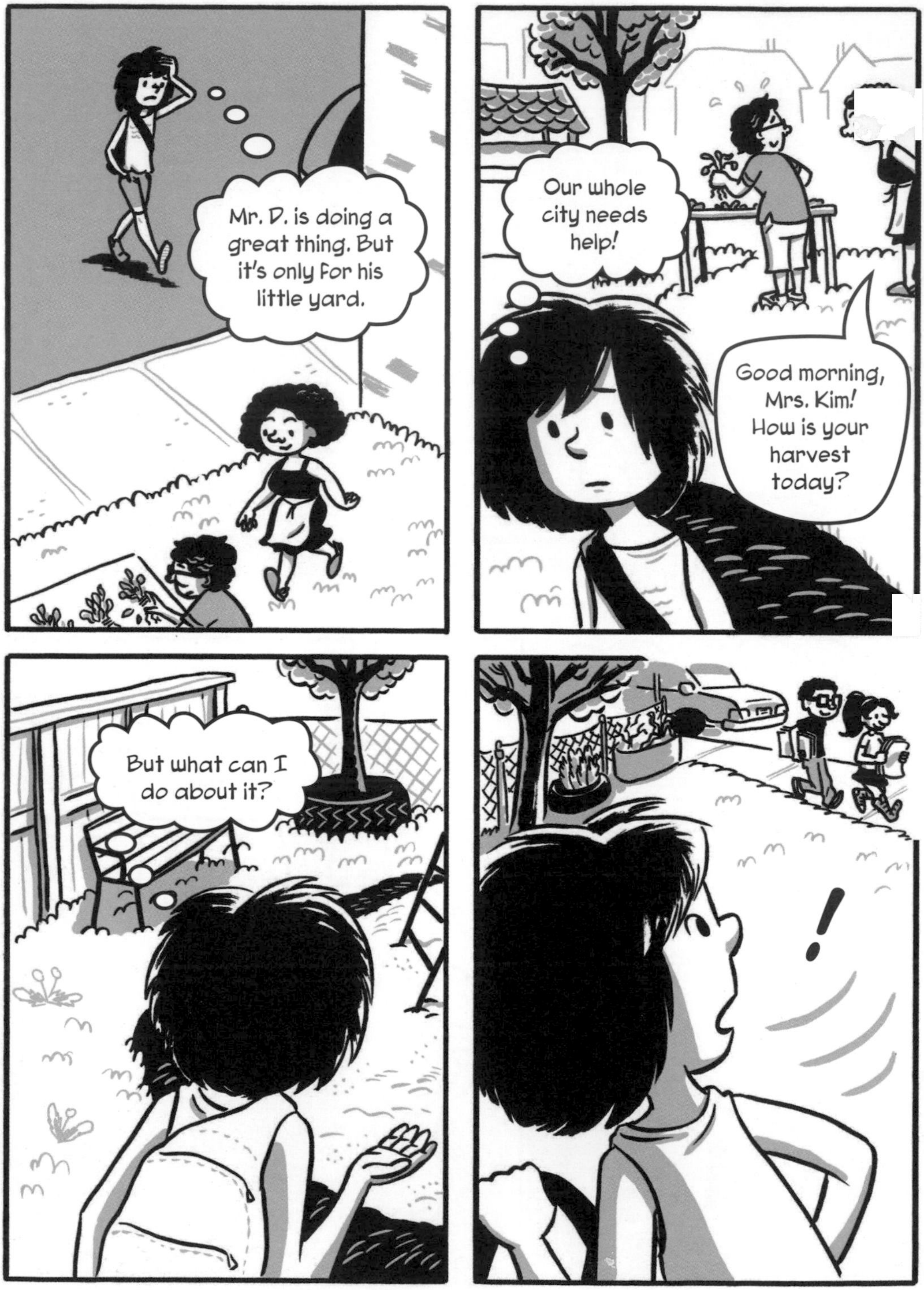
Mr. D. is doing a great thing. But it's only for his little yard.
Our whole city needs help!
Good morning, Mrs. Kim! How is your harvest today?
But what can I do about it?
!

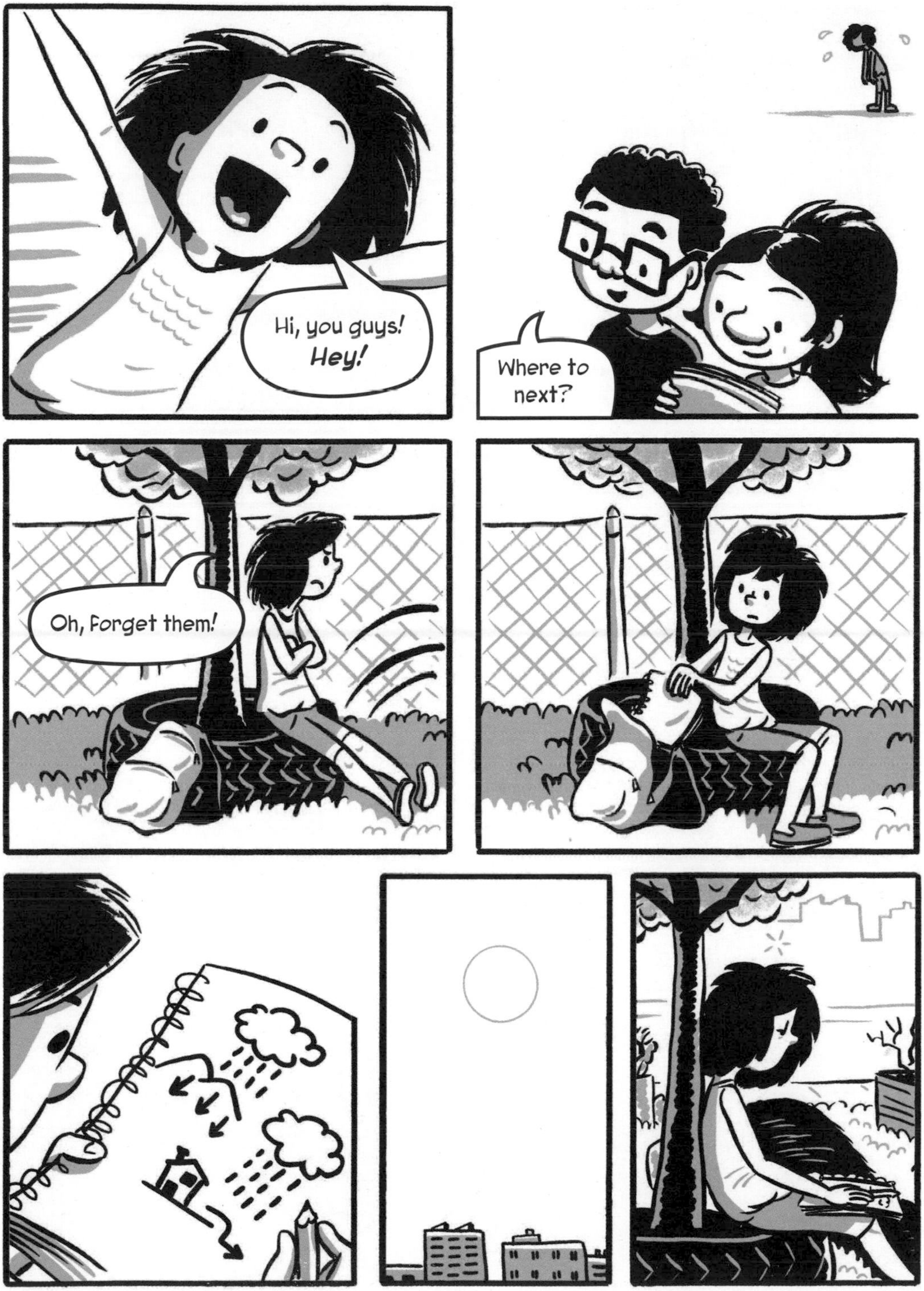
Hi, you guys!
Hey!
Where to next?
Oh, forget them!

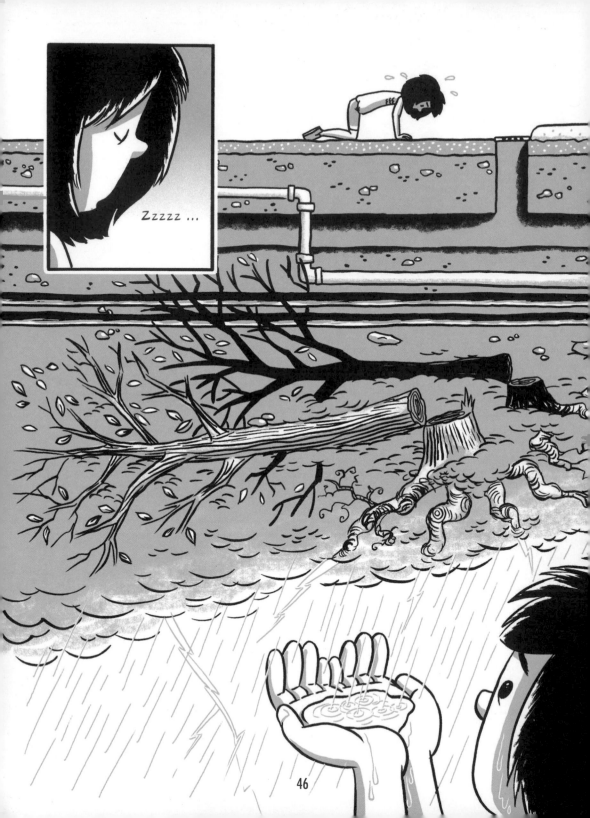

Zzzzz ...

46

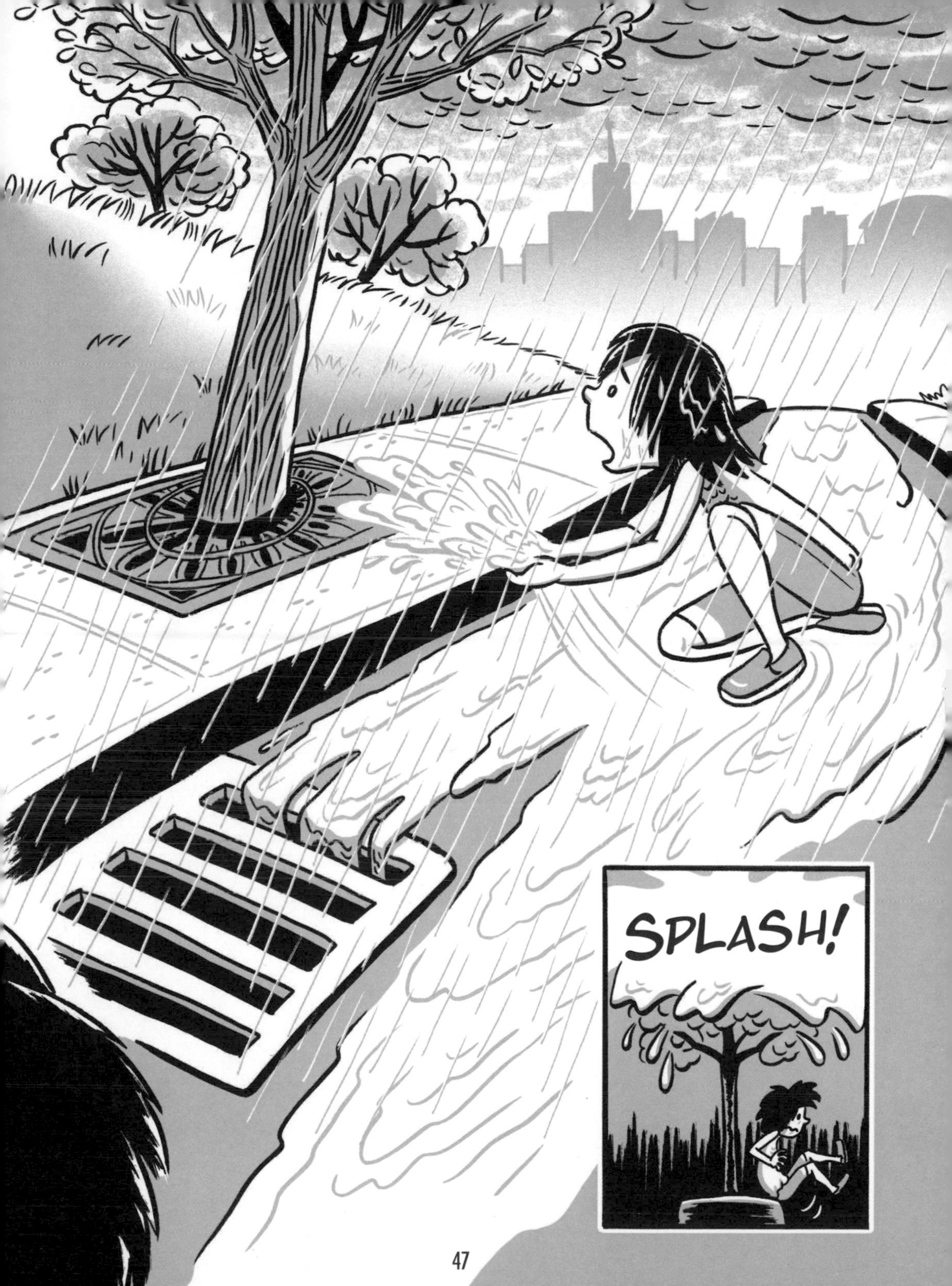
SPLASH!

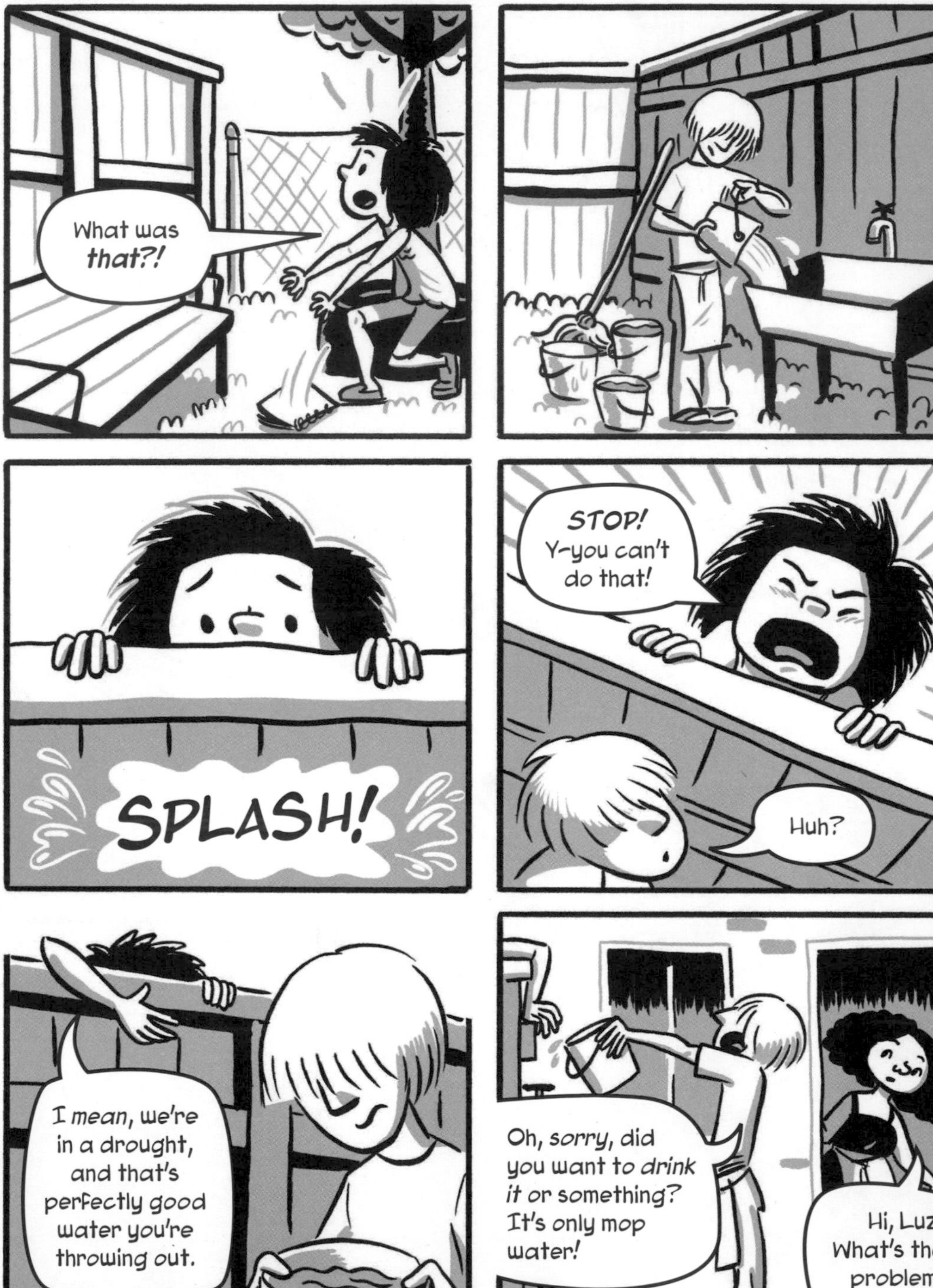
What was *that?!*
SPLASH!
STOP! Y-you can't do that!
Huh?
I *mean*, we're in a drought, and that's perfectly good water you're throwing out.
Oh, *sorry*, did you want to *drink it* or something? It's only mop water!
Hi, Luz. What's the problem, guys?

49

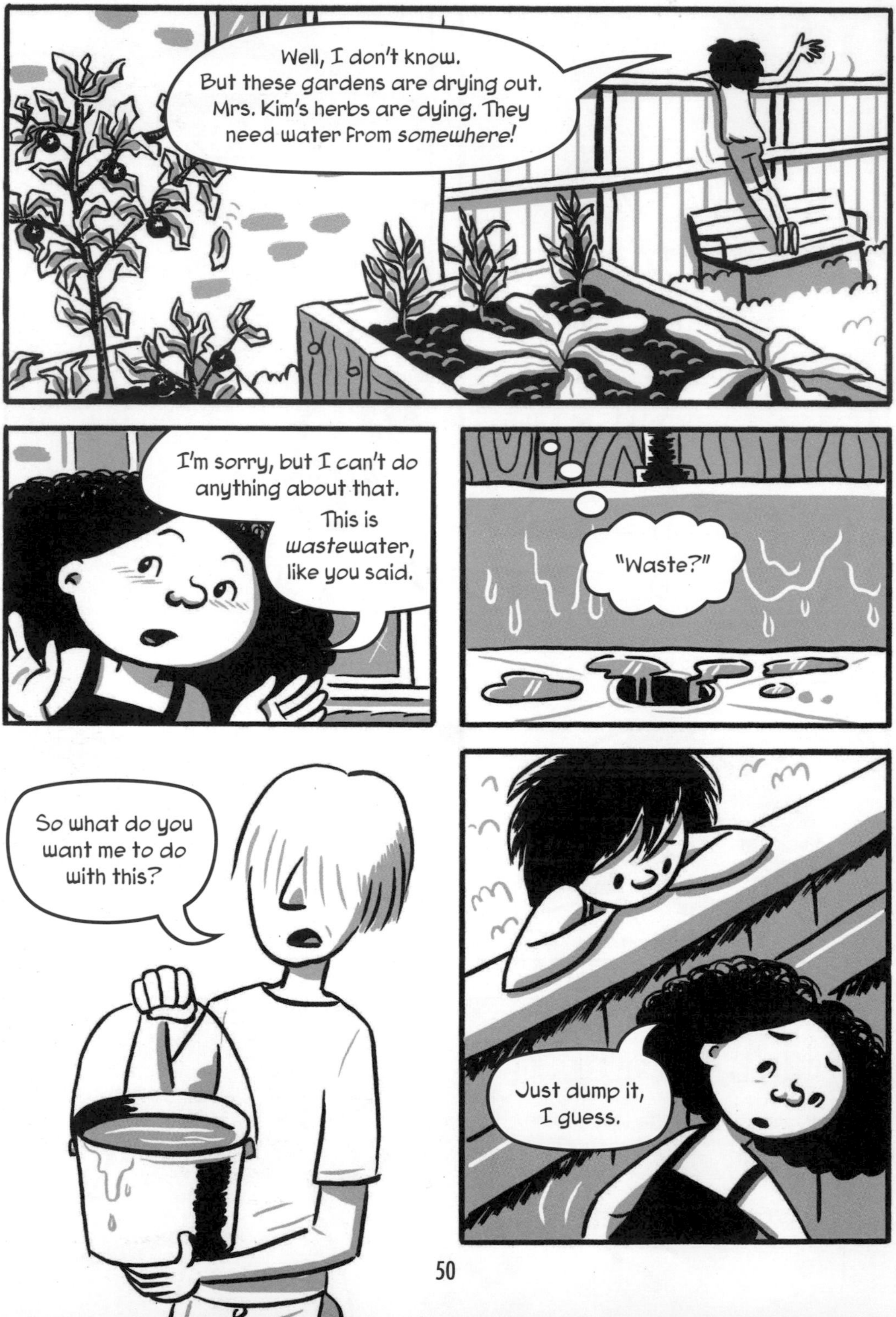
Well, I don't know. But these gardens are drying out. Mrs. Kim's herbs are dying. They need water from *somewhere!*
I'm sorry, but I can't do anything about that.
This is *waste*water, like you said.
"Waste?"
So what do you want me to do with this?
Just dump it, I guess.

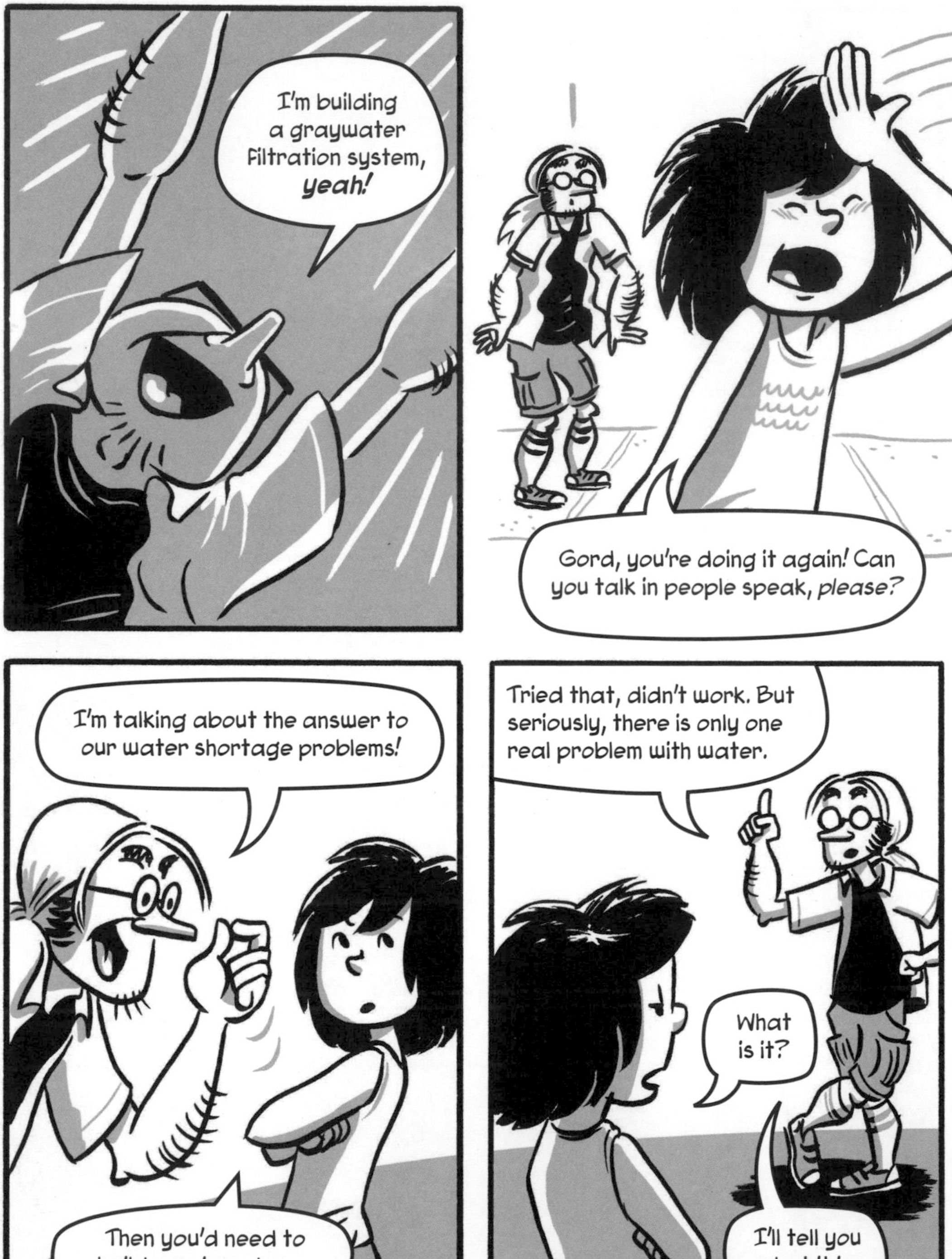
I'm building a graywater filtration system, *yeah!*
Gord, you're doing it again! Can you talk in people speak, *please?*
I'm talking about the answer to our water shortage problems!
Then you'd need to build a rain maker ...
Tried that, didn't work. But seriously, there is only one real problem with water.
What is it?
I'll tell you what it is.

54

BOILING POINT

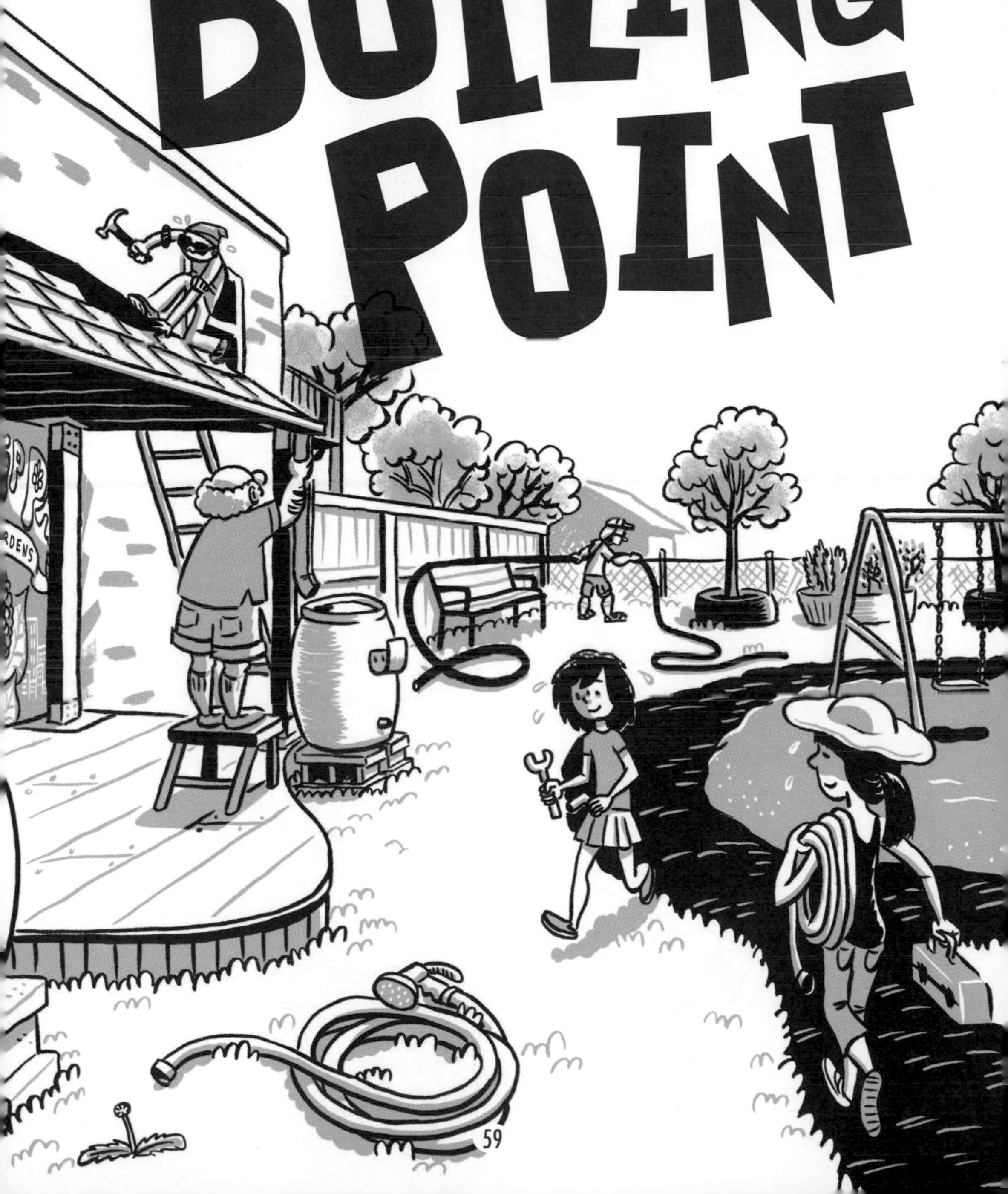

61

65

67

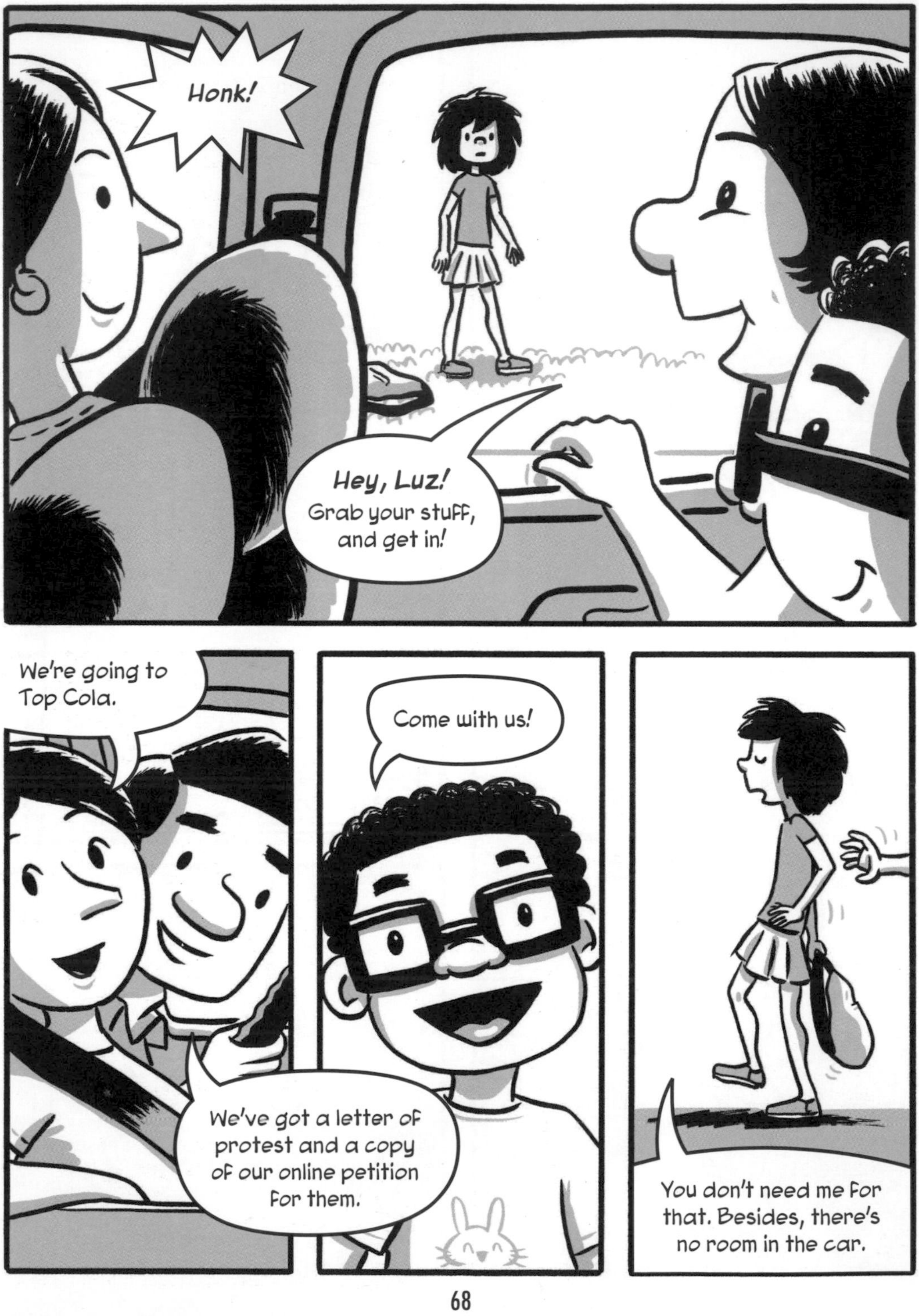

Honk!
Hey, Luz! Grab your stuff, and get in!
We're going to Top Cola.
Come with us!
We've got a letter of protest and a copy of our online petition for them.
You don't need me for that. Besides, there's no room in the car.

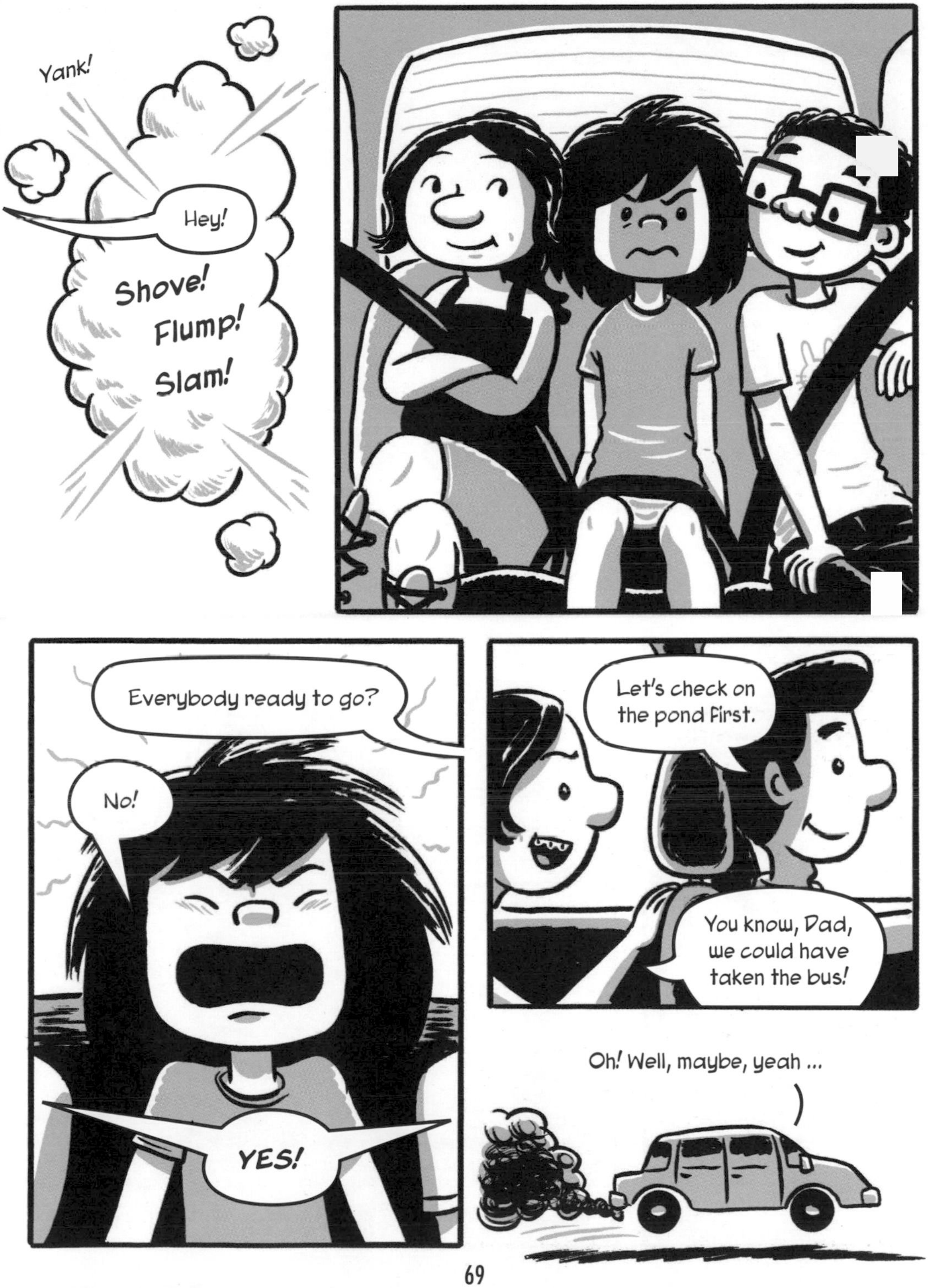
Yank!
Hey!
Shove!
Flump!
Slam!
Everybody ready to go?
No!
YES!
Let's check on the pond first.
You know, Dad, we could have taken the bus!
Oh! Well, maybe, yeah ...

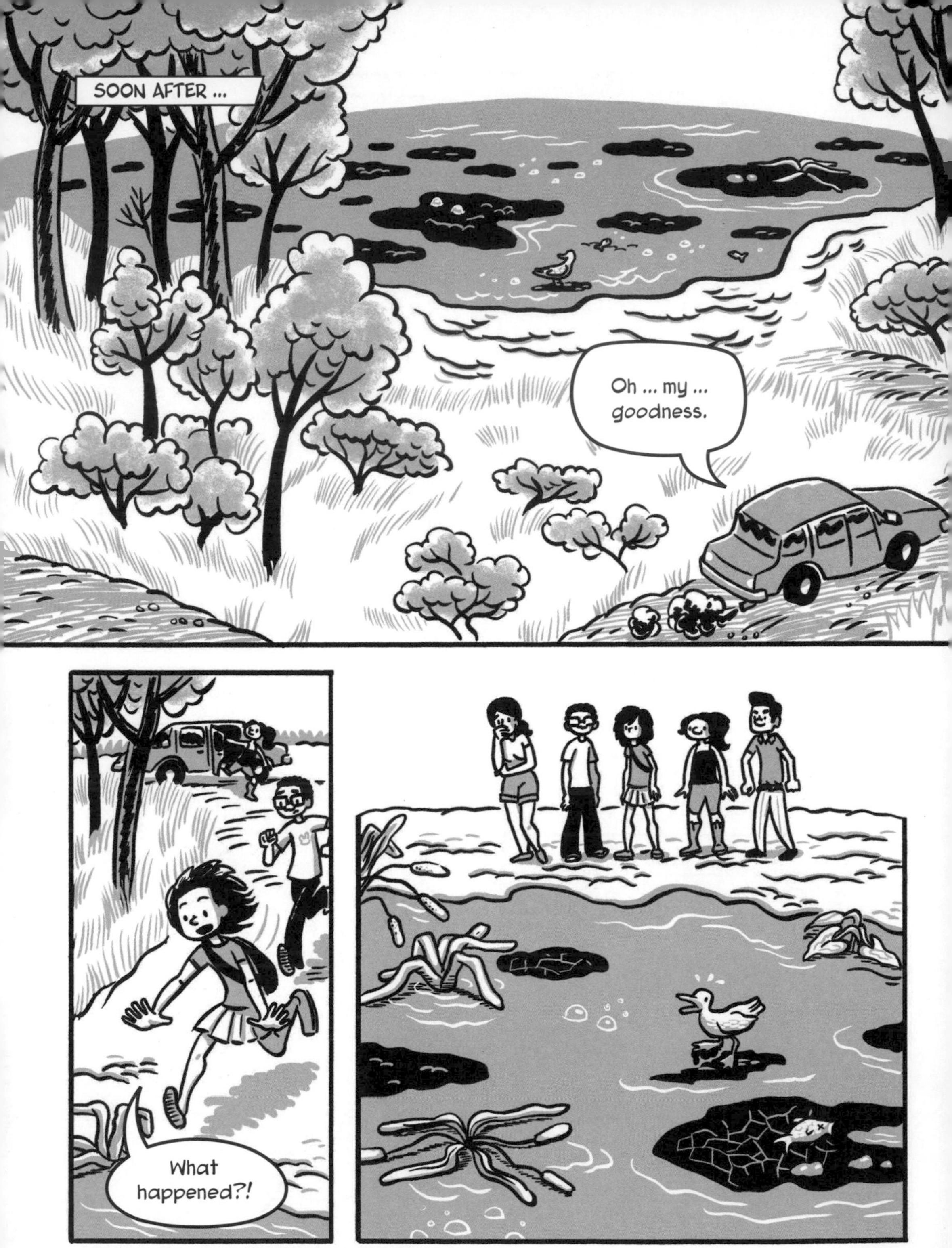
SOON AFTER ...
Oh ... my ... goodness.
What happened?!

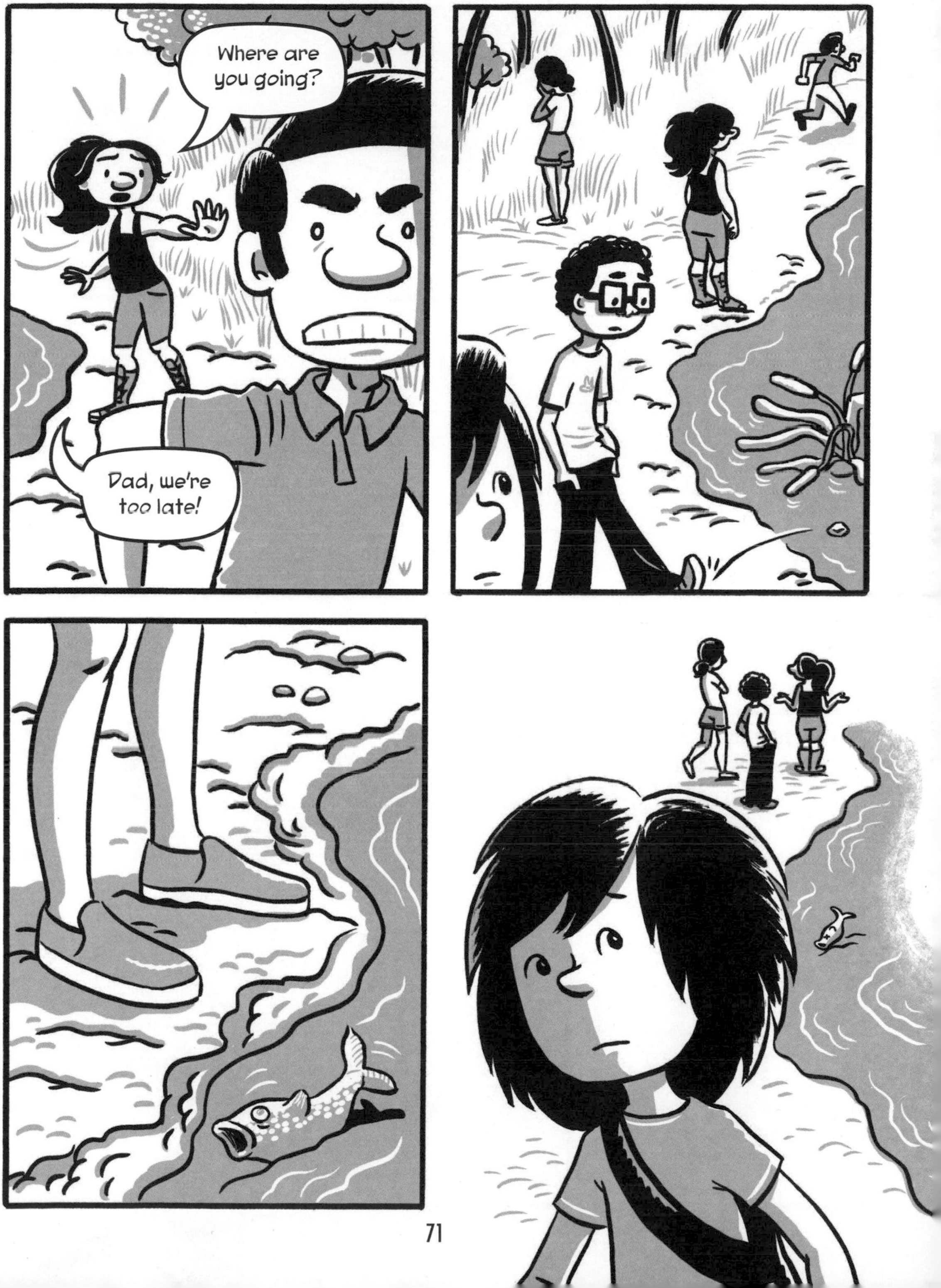
Where are you going?
Dad, we're too late!

72

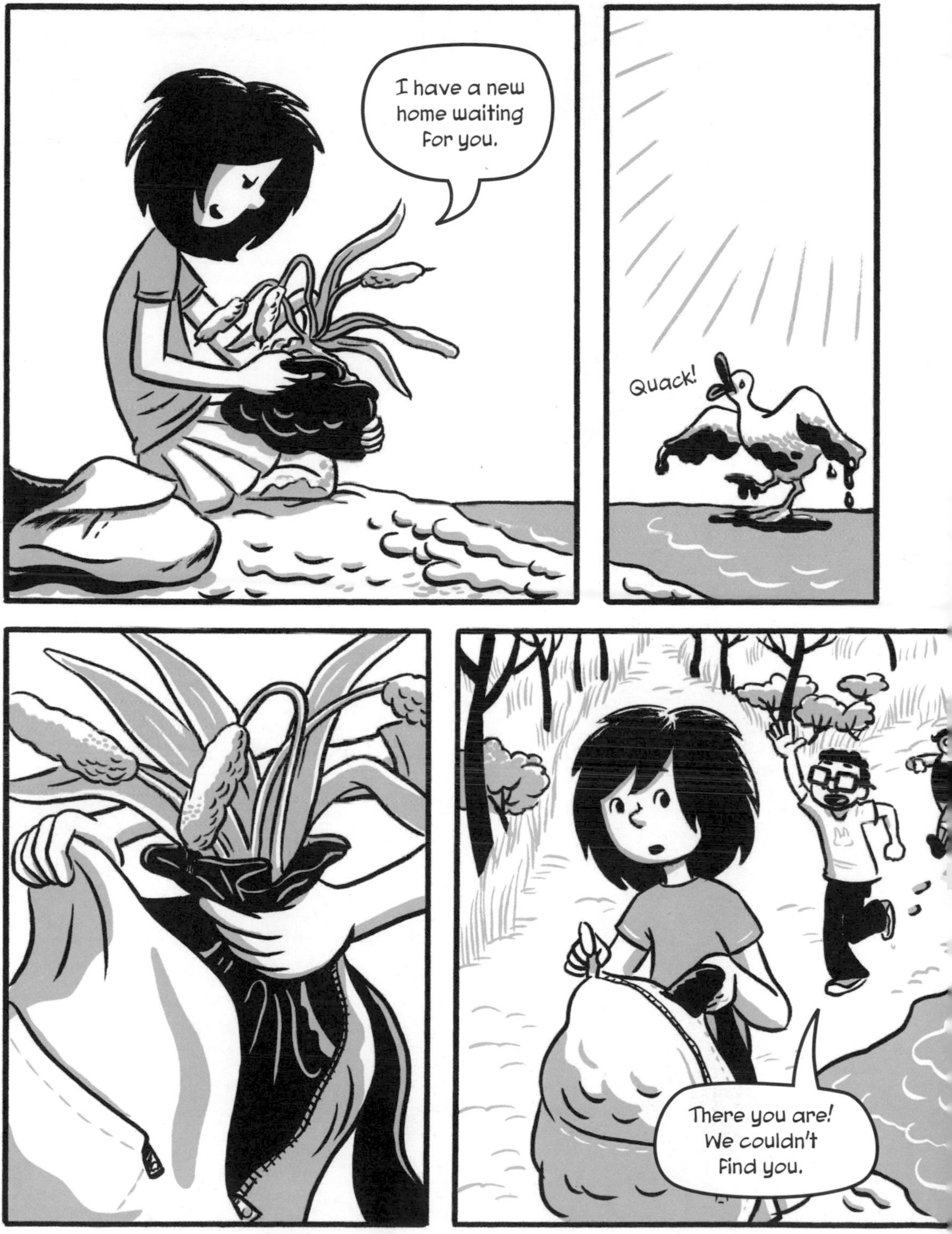
I have a new home waiting for you.
Quack!
There you are! We couldn't find you.

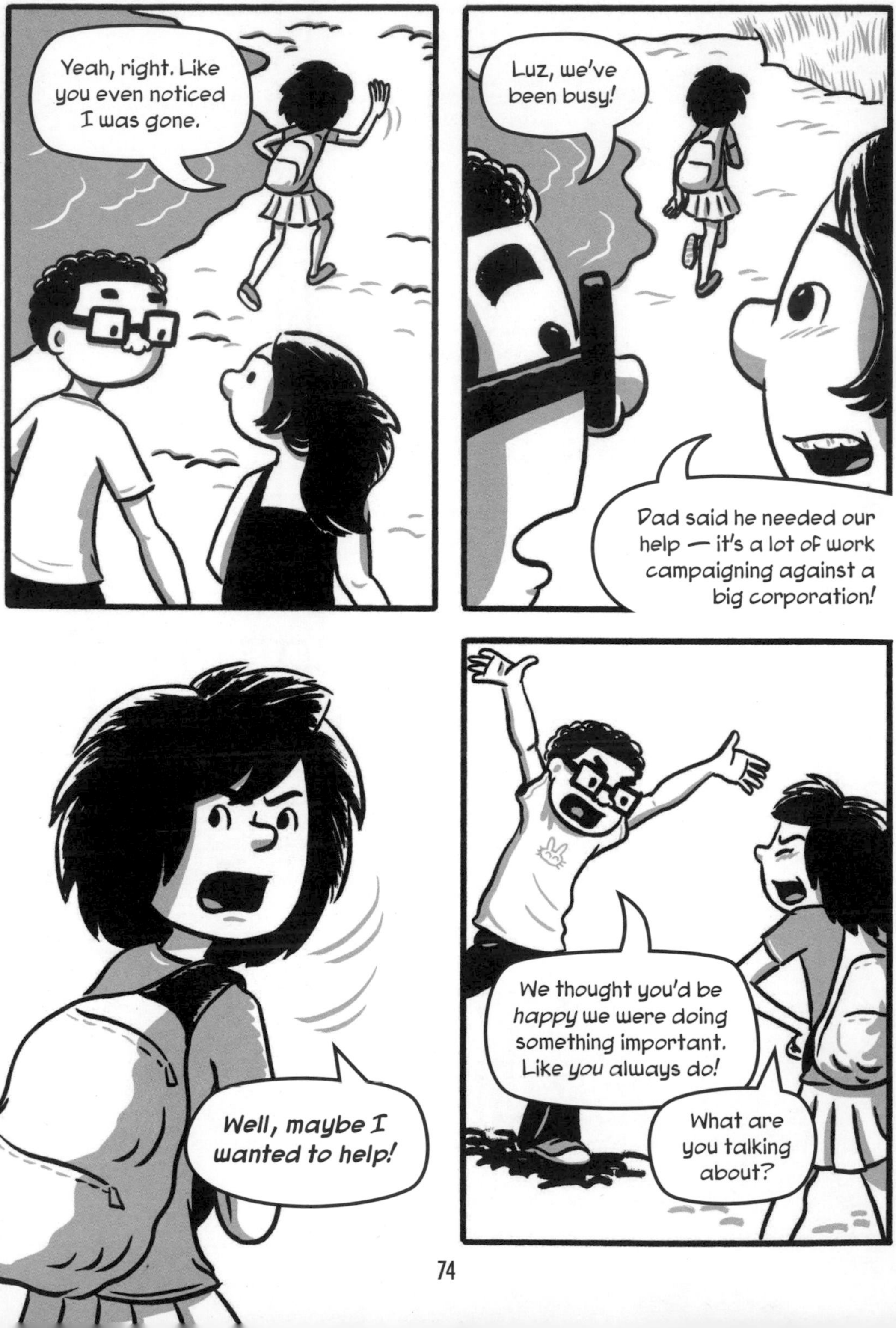
Yeah, right. Like you even noticed I was gone.
Luz, we've been busy!
Dad said he needed our help — it's a lot of work campaigning against a big corporation!
Well, maybe I wanted to help!
We thought you'd be *happy* we were doing something important. Like *you* always do!
What are you talking about?

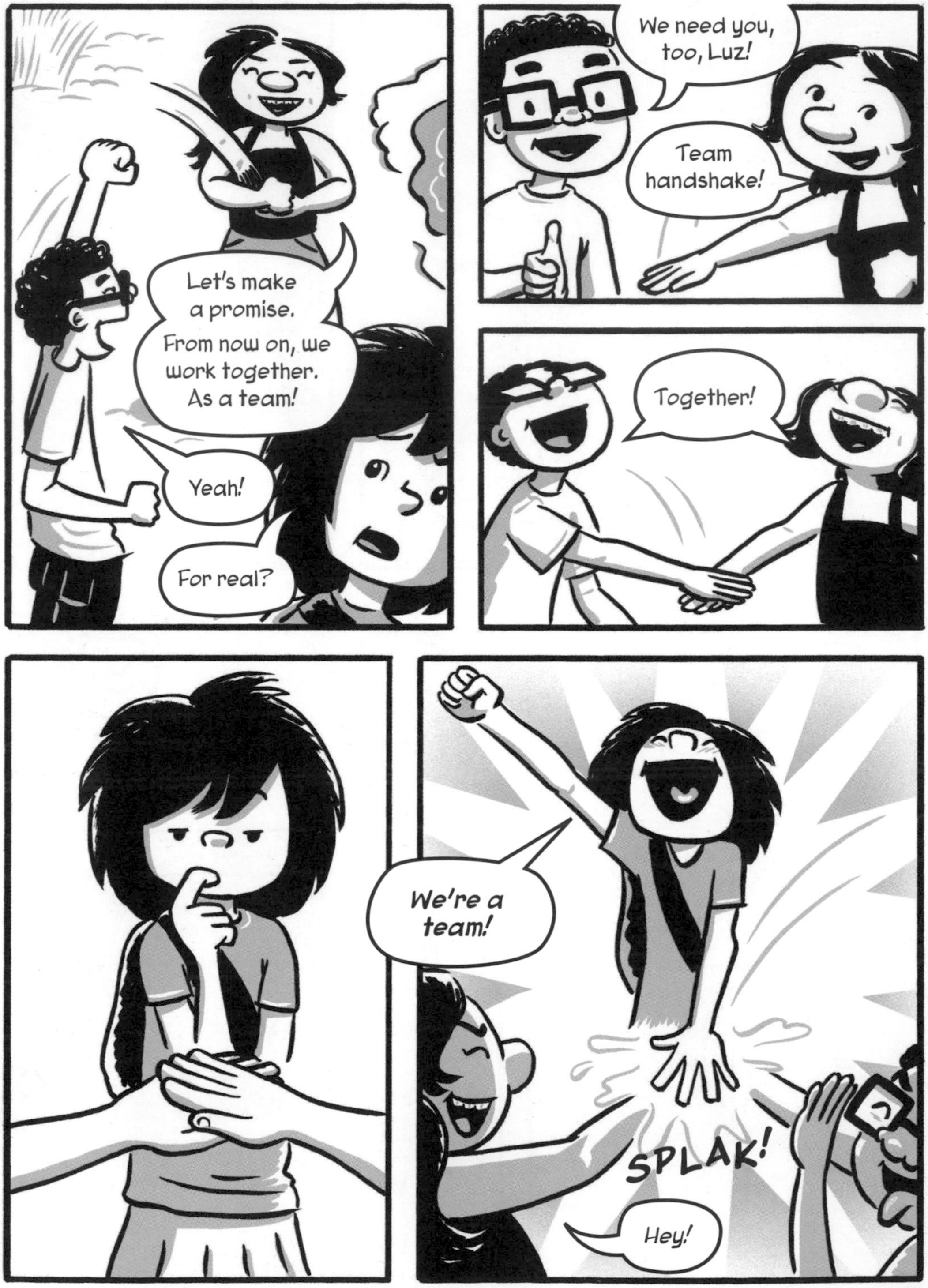
Let's make a promise.
From now on, we work together. As a team!
Yeah!
For real?
We need you, too, Luz!
Team handshake!
Together!
We're a team!
SPLAK!
Hey!

77

78

79

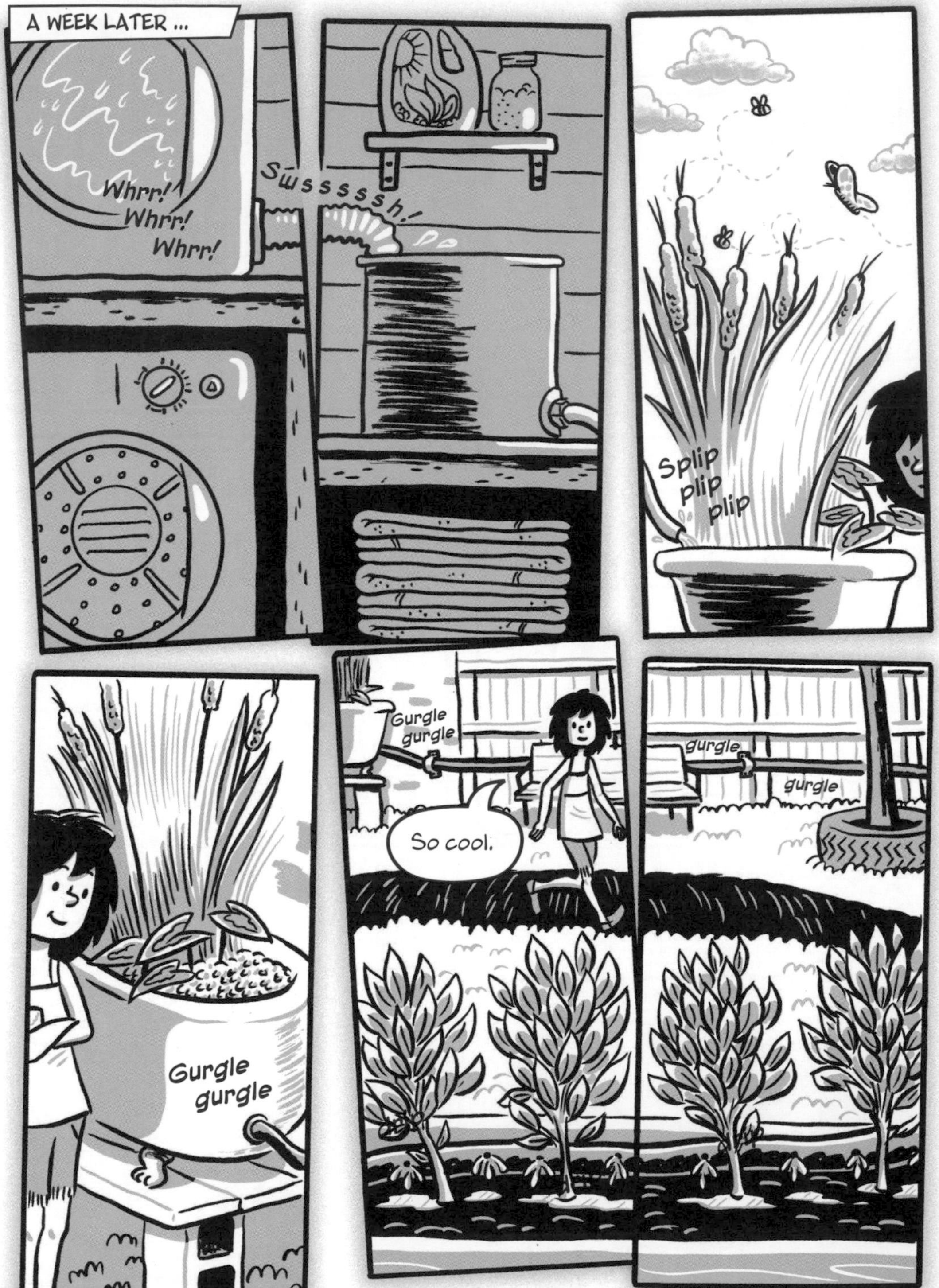
A WEEK LATER ...
Whrr! Whrr! Whrr!
Swsssssh!
Splip plip plip
Gurgle gurgle
Gurgle gurgle
So cool.
gurgle
gurgle

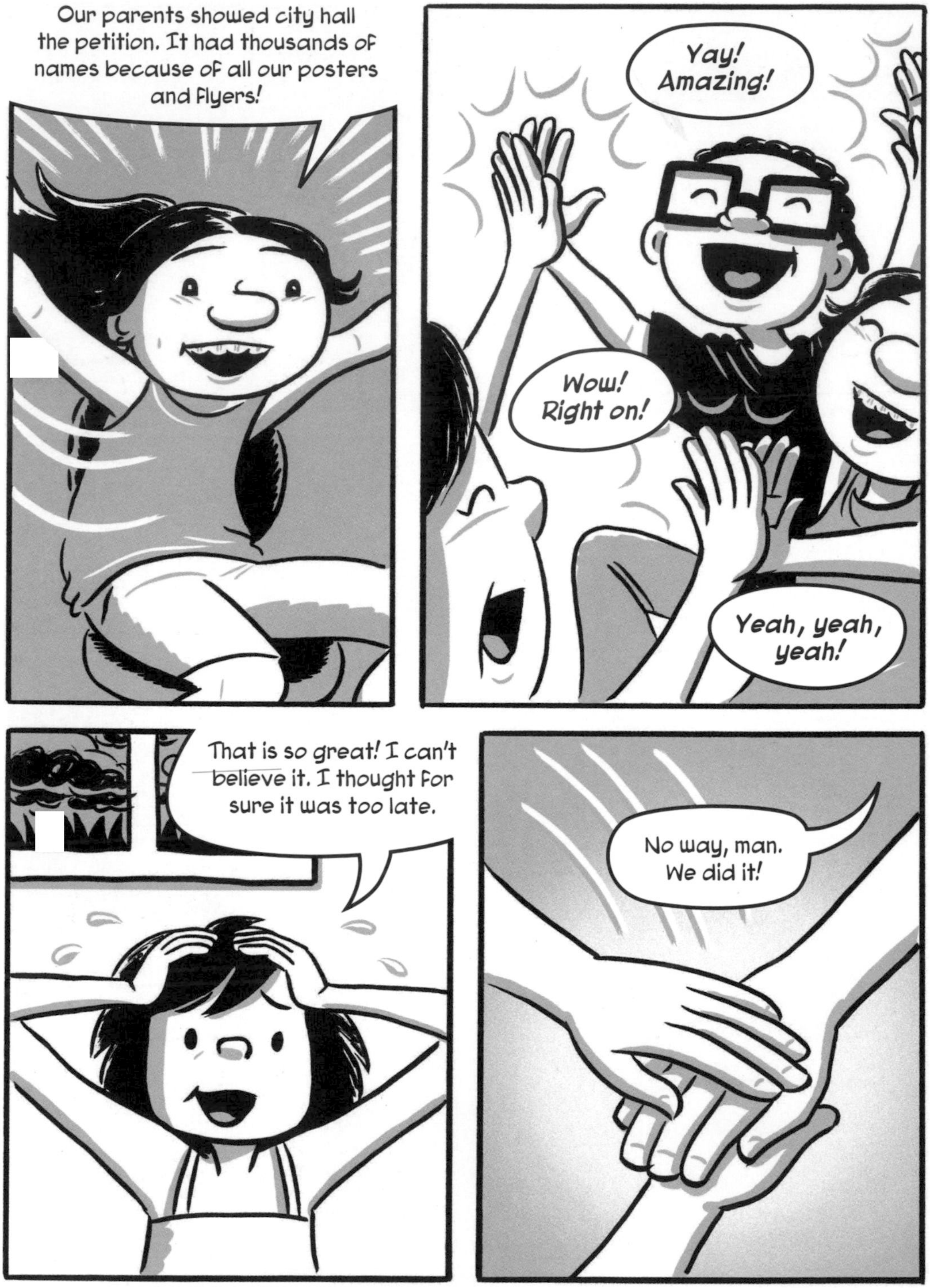
Our parents showed city hall the petition. It had thousands of names because of all our posters and flyers!
Yay! Amazing!
Wow! Right on!
Yeah, yeah, yeah!
That is so great! I can't believe it. I thought for sure it was too late.
No way, man. We did it!

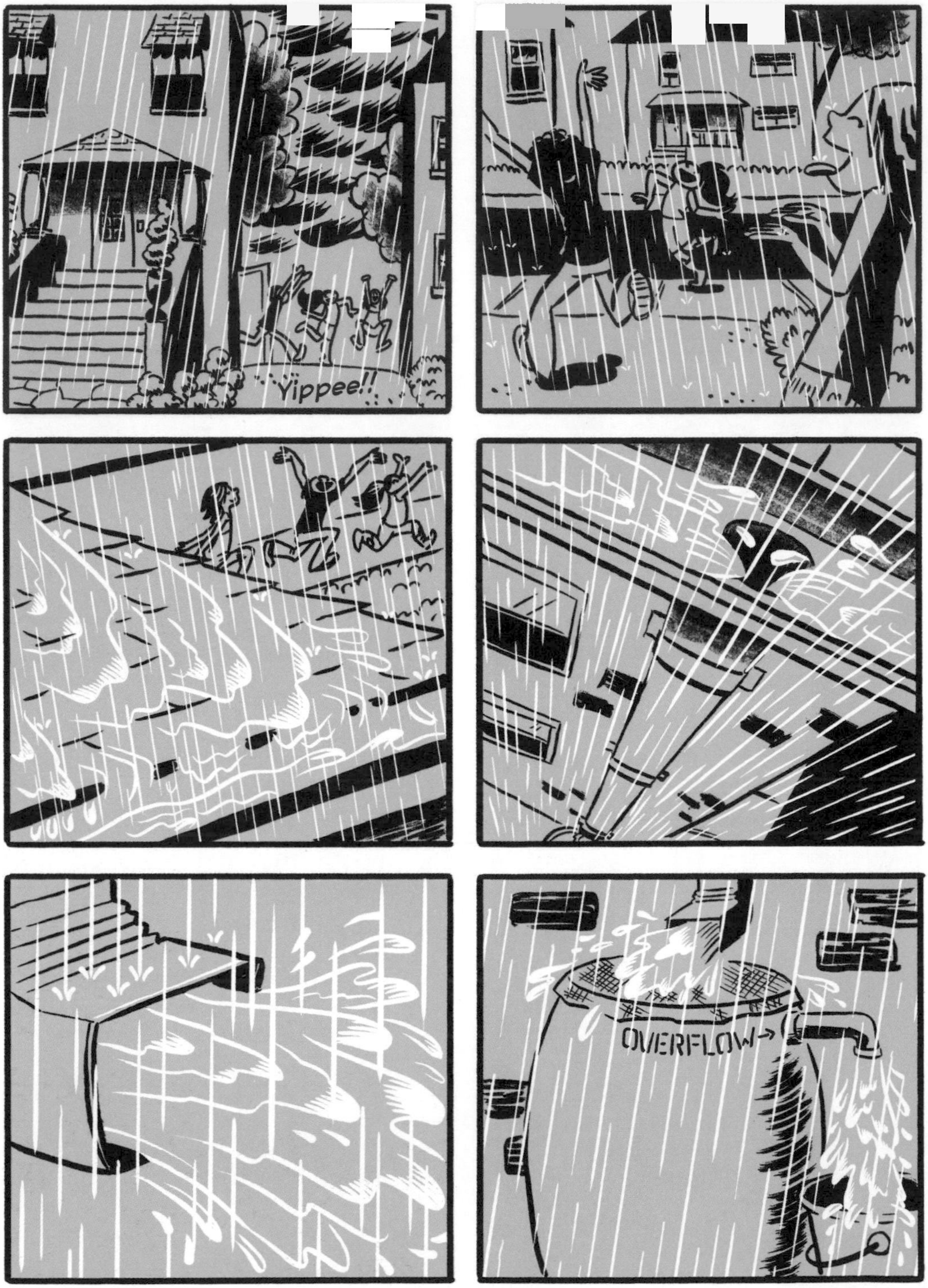
Yippee!!
OVERFLOW→

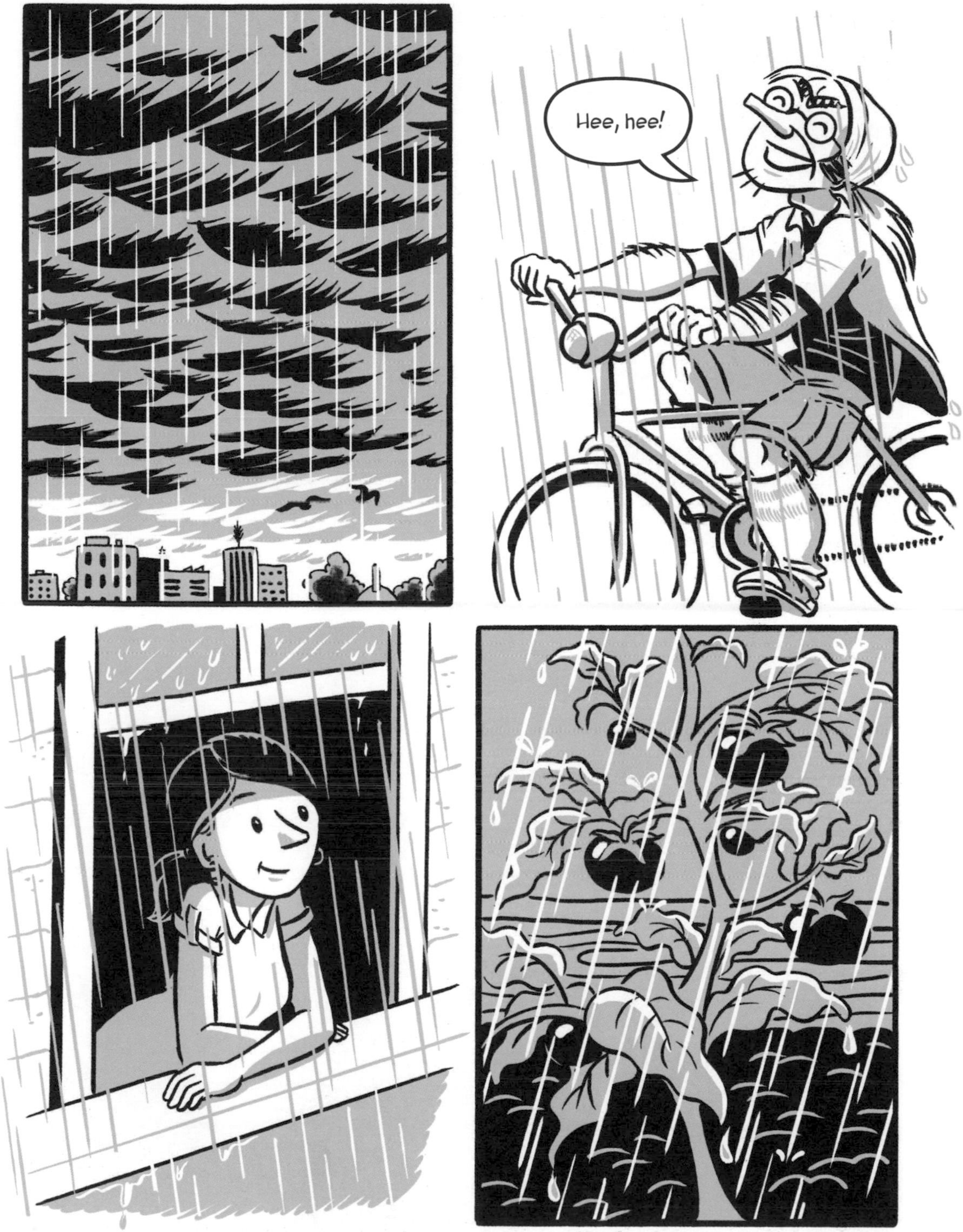
Hee, hee!

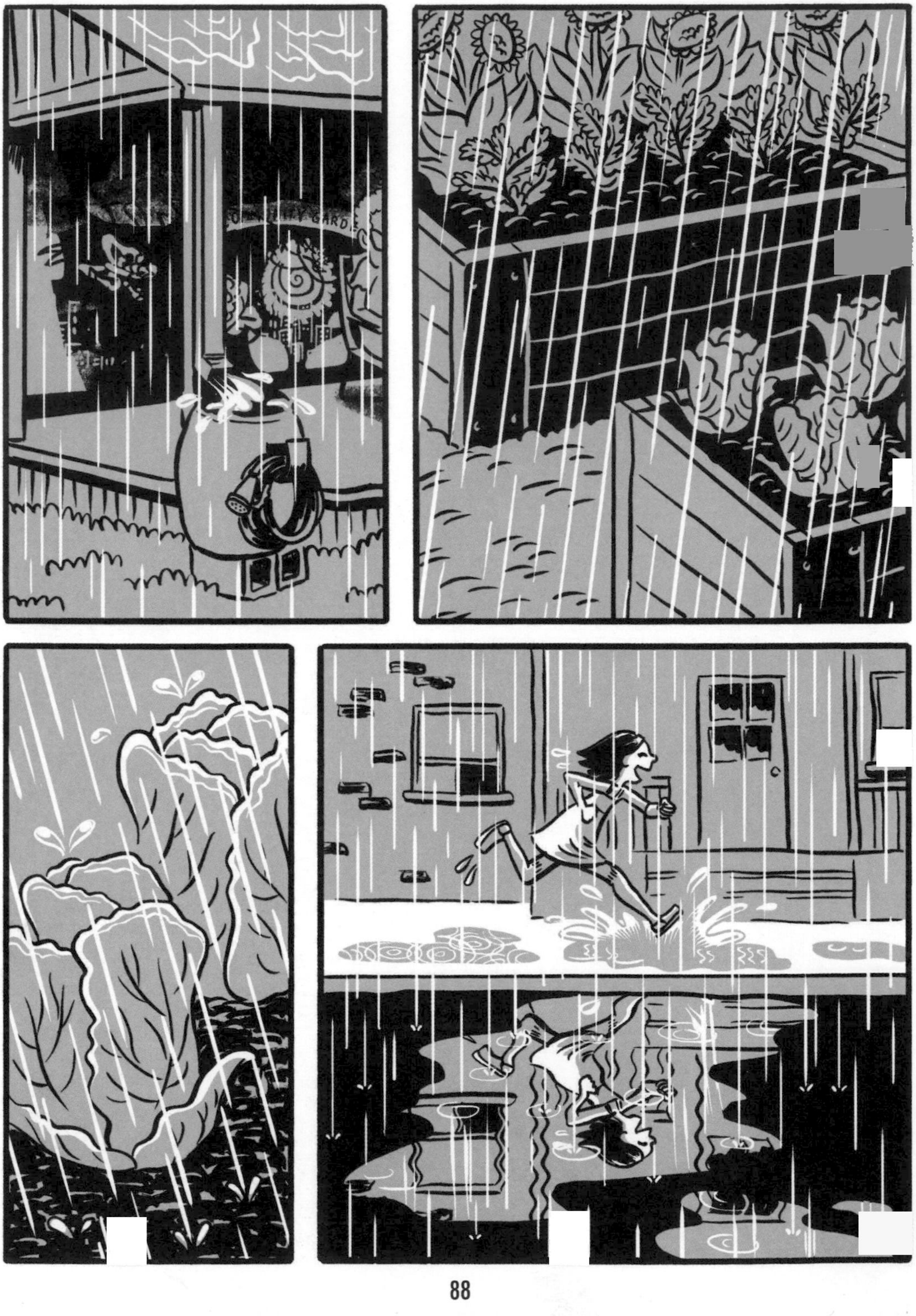

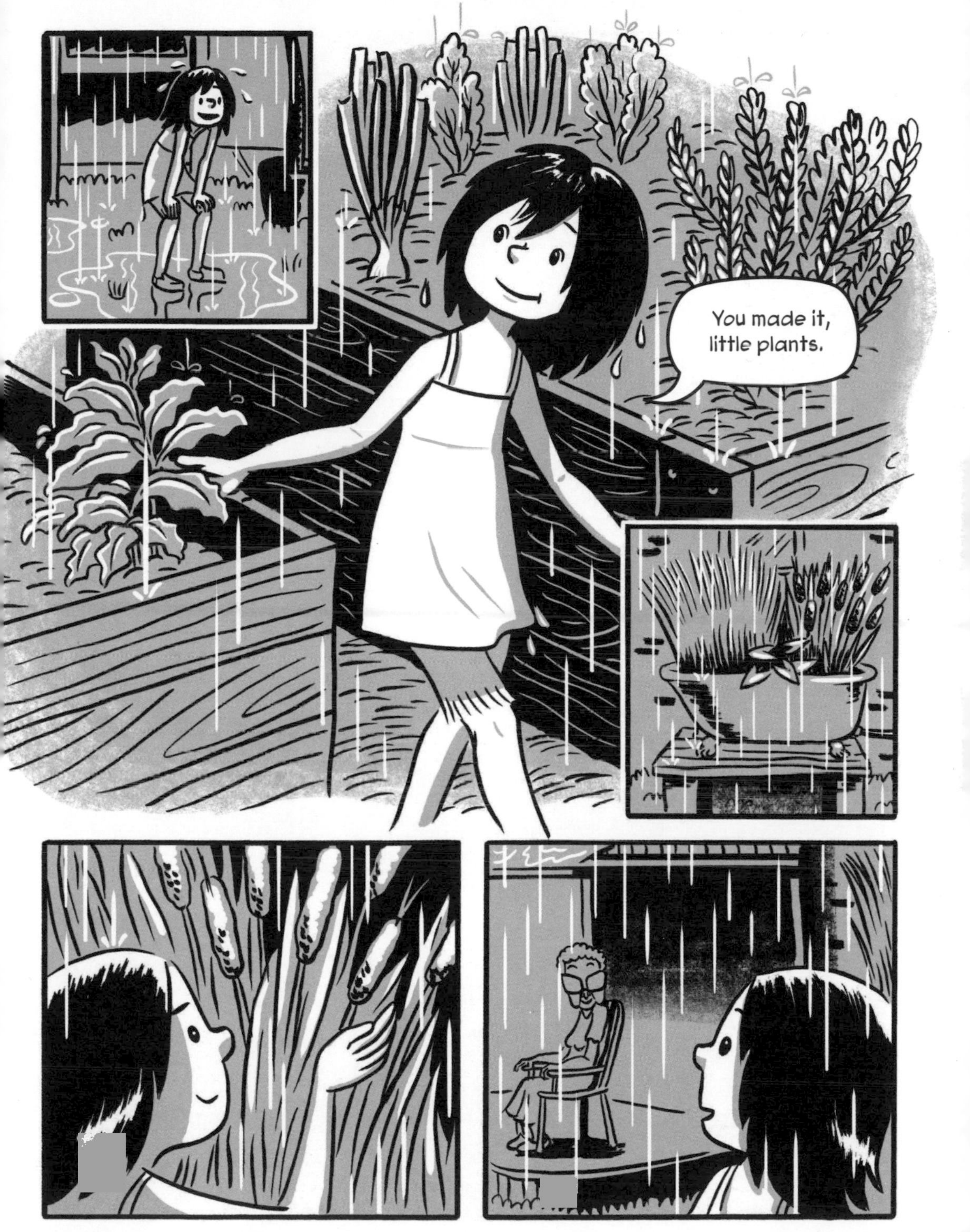
You made it, little plants.

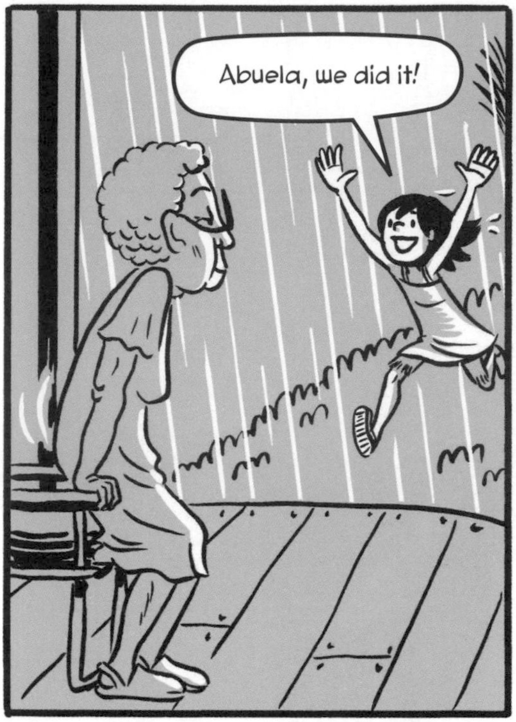
Abuela, we did it!

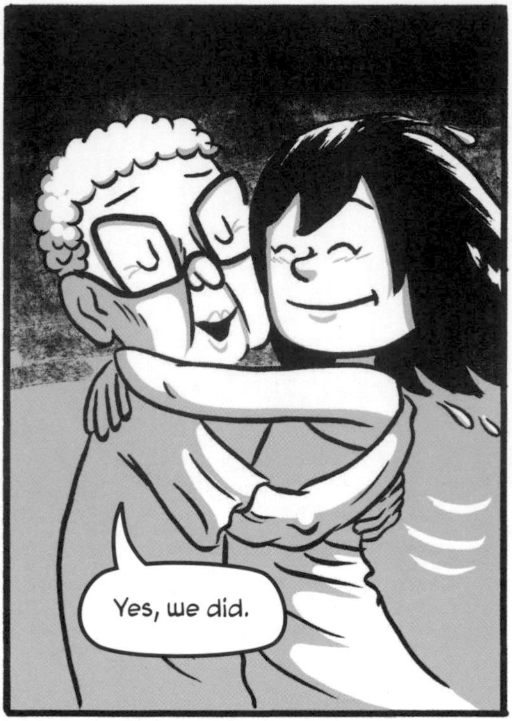
Yes, we did.

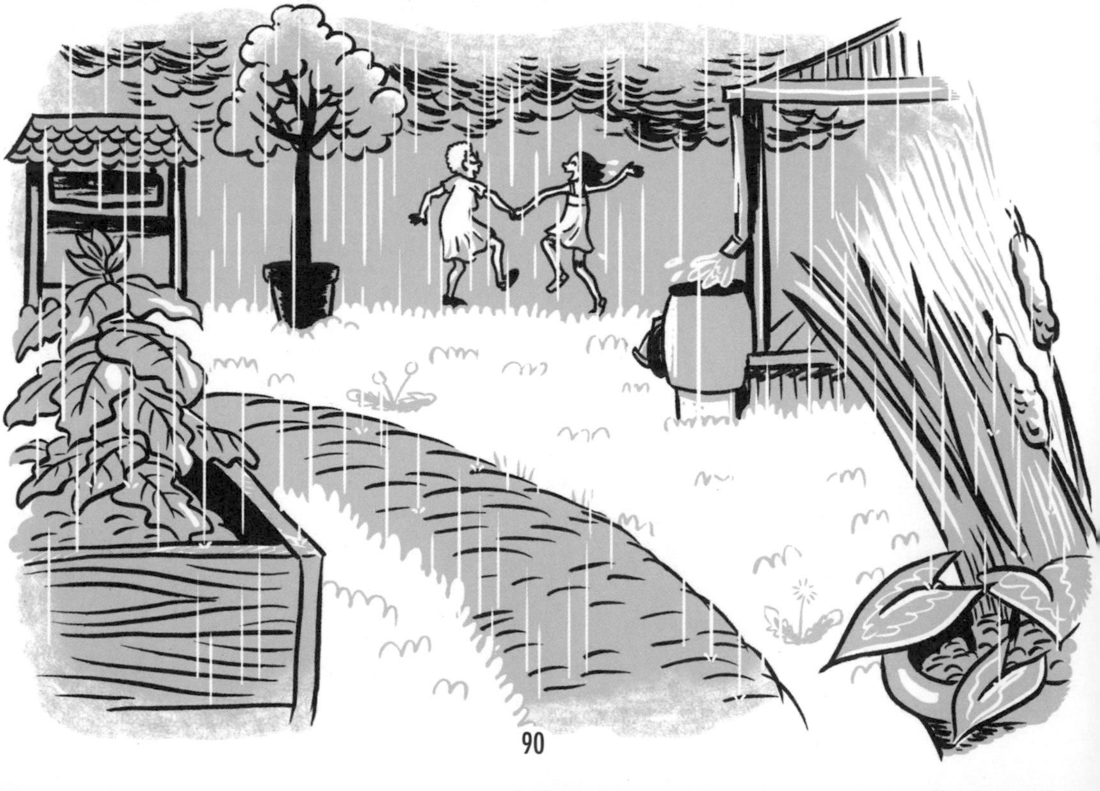

the END

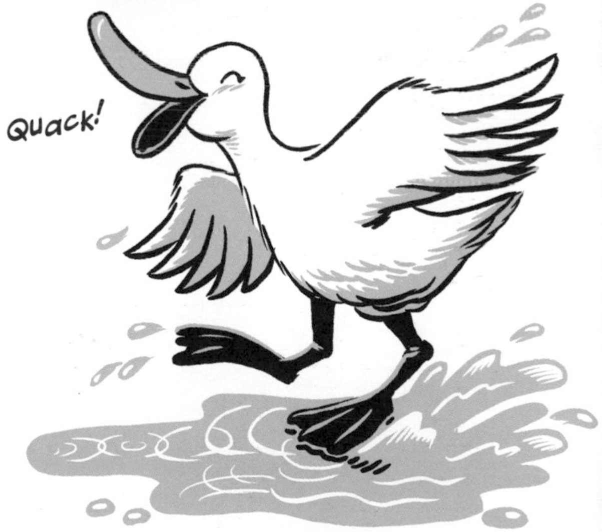
Quack!

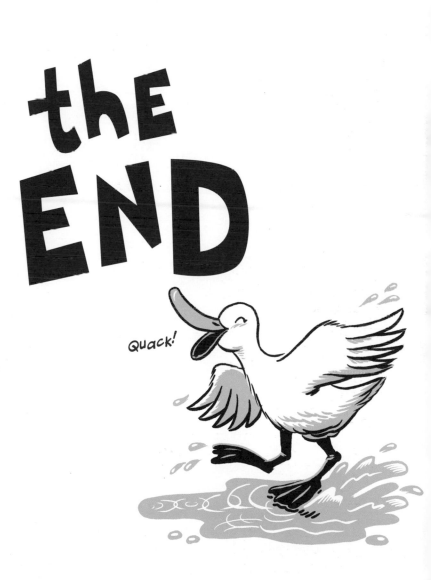

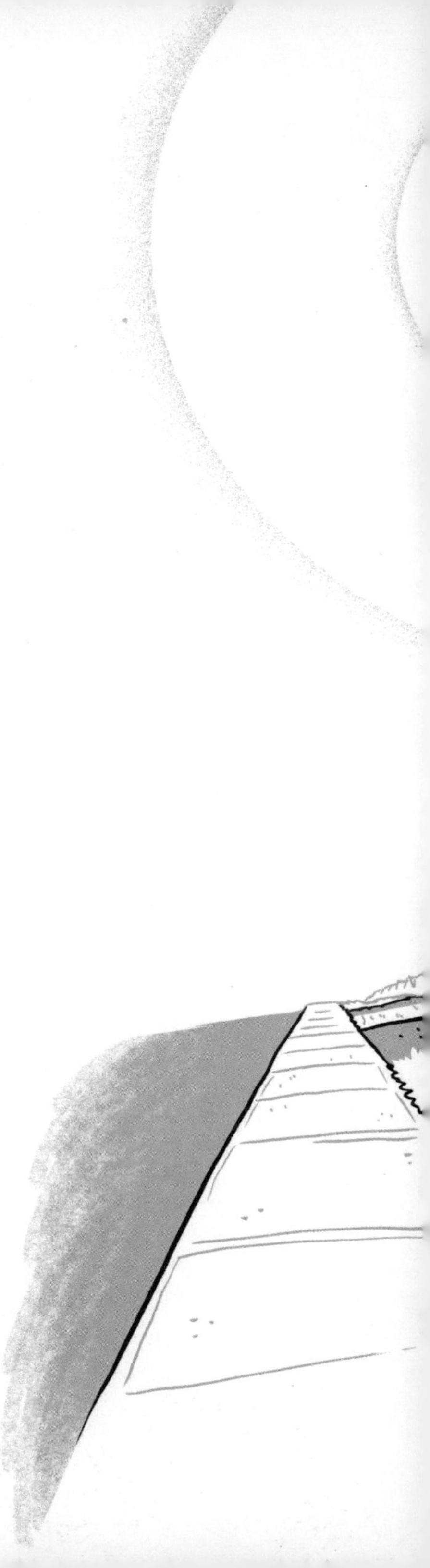

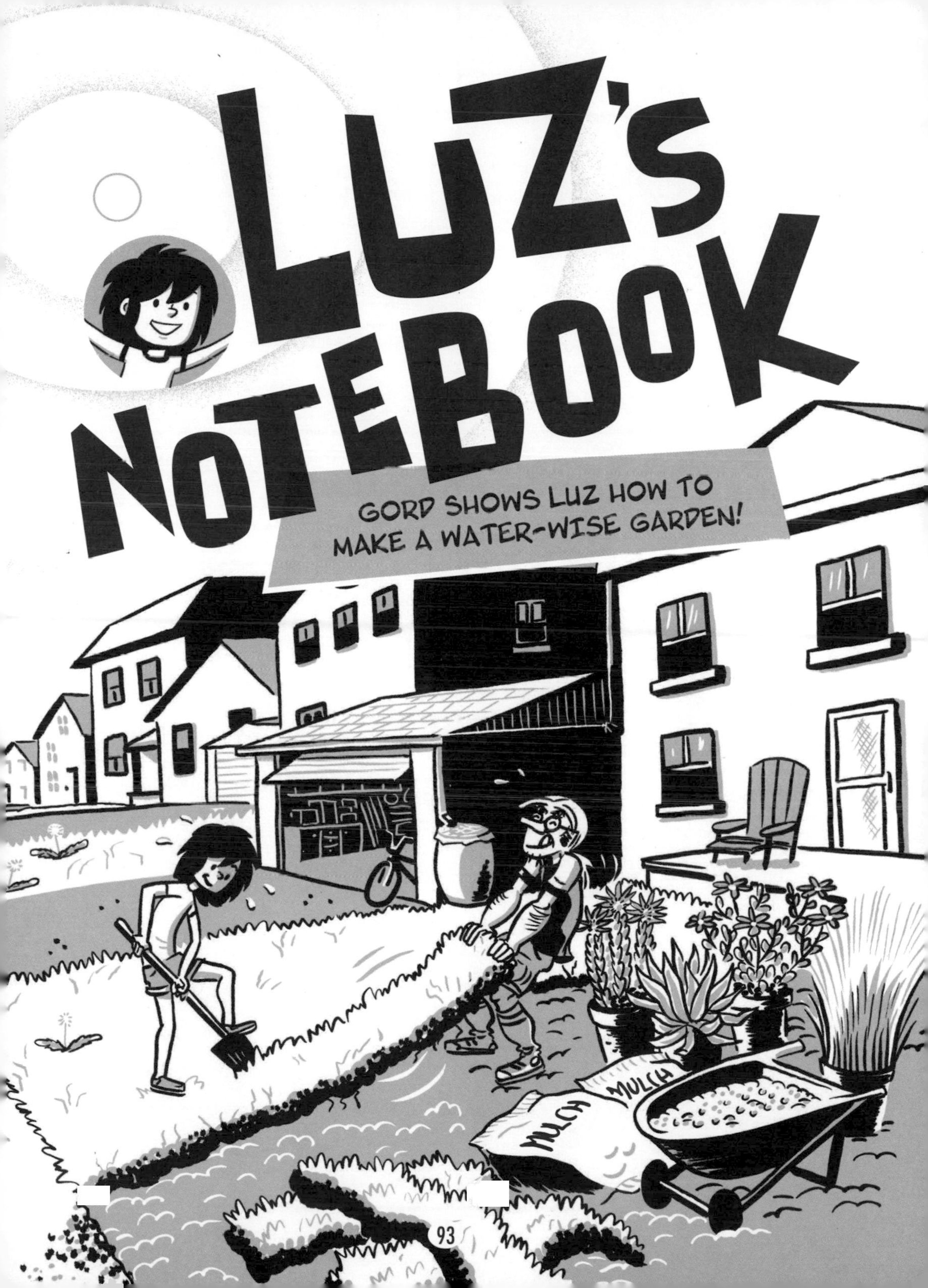
LUZ'S NOTEBOOK
GORD SHOWS LUZ HOW TO MAKE A WATER-WISE GARDEN!
MULCH
MULCH

95

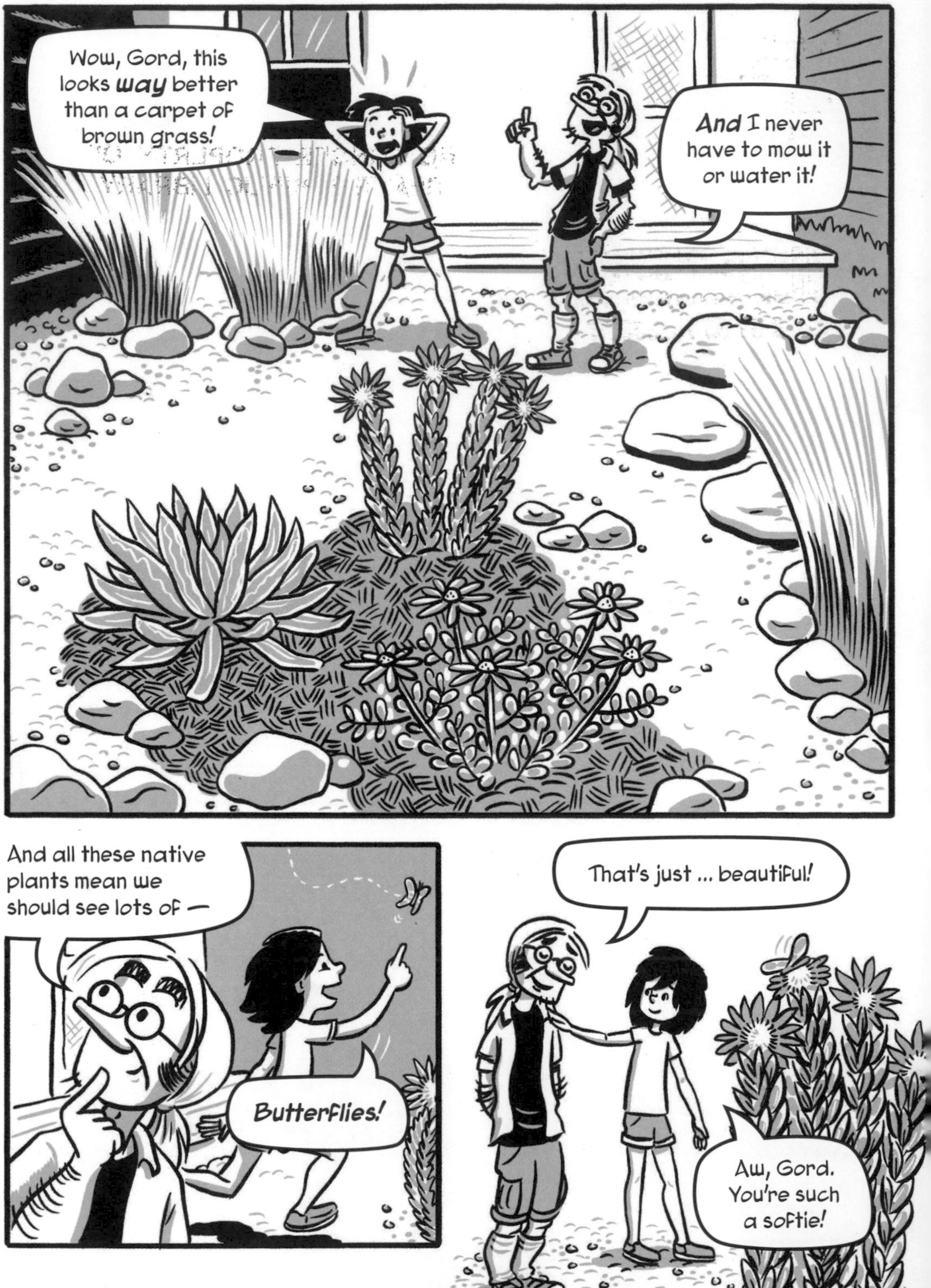
Wow, Gord, this looks *way* better than a carpet of brown grass!
And I never have to mow it or water it!
And all these native plants mean we should see lots of —
Butterflies!
That's just ... beautiful!
Aw, Gord. You're such a softie!